MW01596314

Anna and Alfred

Jake Spencer Reports

Lizbeth Murphy

authorHOUSE®

AuthorHouse™
1663 Liberty Drive
Bloomington, IN 47403
www.authorhouse.com
Phone: 1-800-839-8640

First published by AuthorHouse 6/29/2009

ISBN: 978-1-4389-7956-4 (e)
ISBN: 978-1-4389-7955-7 (sc)

Printed in the United States of America
Bloomington, Indiana

This book is printed on acid-free paper.

Anna's Story

The book is written in the form of Jake Spencer, a journalist, interviewing an elderly lady in an assisted-living facility. Octogenarians have a wealth of memories locked away in their brains. It behooves journalists to enter senior-citizen facilities in an attempt to release some of those memories. Residents could be interviewed in an effort to capture some of those gems before dementia deprives them of their ability to bring to the fore the many things they have experienced in life.

Jake visited the facility and interviewed old Anna on different days. She unfolded stories of her past. He would take notes. When she grew tired, he would leave quietly and return another day.

The story reveals memories Anna recalled from her past. It served as a reminder to struggling underprivileged youth that there is a way out of their dilemma. If they need guidance, they should seek help. They can and will succeed if they set goals for themselves and strive to attain those goals.

Alfred's Story

Alfred's story reveals the fact that he was born to a teenage mother who decided to keep her child. As the story unfolds, one wonders if her decision was a wise one (due to her immaturity). Her lifestyle may have been a detriment to his emotional well being.

Alfred's mother may have experienced strong maternal feelings for her unborn child as she nurtured him in her womb. She declined any suggestion that she place her baby up for adoption at birth. She honestly believed she could rear her child with all of the love and guidance needed. However, she lacked the ability to make mature decisions.

As the story unwinds, we find that her desperate desire to have a husband superseded her need to rear her child in a loving environment in which he would feel loved and wanted. She married a man who was not the child's father and who displayed very little paternal feelings to Anna's son.

The couple's fun-loving lifestyle and their deep commitment to the children they had together may have caused them to not see how young Alfred was suffering emotionally.

CHAPTER 1

There was a small town in suburban Pennsylvania, where at one time, the community was comprised of mostly upscale Caucasian families. While many employed live-in maids, butlers, janitors, gardeners, and chauffeurs, others had cleaning ladies who usually traveled daily from surrounding areas and returned home in the evenings by public transportation.

There was a very large apartment building just off of Lancaster Pike in Radnor Township, surrounded by a courtyard where there were lovely single-family homes.

In the janitor's quarters of the apartment building lived an elderly couple, their niece, her husband, and a little girl whose name was Anna. The year was in 1930. Anna was about six years old. She was the only African-

American child in her class. All of the teachers in that school were white at the time.

One day, little Anna sat at her desk, waving her right hand frantically, trying to attract the attention of Miss Rachael, who seemed to be ignoring the little girl. Finally, she looked in Anna's direction and said, "I will get to you in a minute." The small teary-eyed girl wriggled and squirmed in her seat. Being an obedient child, she would not get up without the teacher's permission.

Suddenly, she lost control of her bladder. Urine flowed profusely, saturating her clothing and pouring out of the seat onto the floor. Her classmates around her giggled and pointed to the wet floor. Only then did Miss Rachael notice her student's dilemma. She responded with an almost inaudible, "Oh my God."

Wet, humiliated, and crying, Anna rose to her feet and immediately left the classroom. She went out of the school and across busy Lancaster Pike. Drivers blew horns and swerved their automobiles in an attempt to avoid striking the little girl.

Upon reaching home—wet, crying, and traumatized by nearly being killed—she told her great aunt what happened. The older woman then told her employers in the building of the situation.

Word spread among the apartment residents. A group of mothers visited the school. They voiced their complaints to the school principal, who summoned the teacher.

Miss Rachel was reprimanded. She had to apologize to Anna and explain to her students that what had occurred was not Anna's fault. She explained that this situation could have happened to any one of them.

At that time, Republican President Herbert Hoover was in his final years in office. He defeated Alfred Smith of New York in 1928. Then in 1933, Franklin D. Roosevelt became president and remained in that office until 1945.

At that time, there were concerns pertaining to race and religion. Still, some people cared about equal rights and fair treatment of minorities. This is not to imply that all Caucasians in that beautiful county believed in equal rights. Many chose to live in that area because they preferred to live apart from others whom they deemed undesirable.

Anna's parents were high school classmates who married at a very early age. They argued frequently. She remembered a few nice things about her dad. He hugged her a lot and took her places. She loved him. She did recall the times she rode in his Model T Ford automobile. (Then again, it may have been a Model A; she did not remember.) She recalled seeing her father use a hand crank in front of the car to start the motor. He would at times make two or three turns, which started the ignition. He yelled, "Come on, Anna Let's go!" Those were happy times; she never forgot how much she enjoyed riding in the rumble seat, as it was called in those days. That seat could be reached by pulling down a door in the back of the car (where a modern-day car would have a trunk). It could seat two people. To get into it, one had to climb up on a step on the fender and climb into the seat.

There were no seat belts. That car never would pass inspection in modern times. Had they gone over a high bump, Anna could have been thrown into the roadway. Then again, they were unable to go at excessive rates of speed.

One day, Anna's father was standing in the hallway by the front door, his luggage in hand. He embraced his little daughter and told her that he had to go away. She asked when he would return. He said only that he would be away for a very long time and for her to be a good girl. Anna cried as she watched him walk away, never to see him again.

Her father's departure left a huge void in her life. It was her very first heartbreak, and there were many more to follow. Many years later, when the adult Anna tried to locate her father, she was shown a death certificate. He had died at the age of forty in a Mid-western state.

Anna lived in the apartment with her mother, Sue, and her aunt Janie and uncle Luke. Aunt Janie was Sue's father's sister. She weighed more than two hundred pounds. When she spoke, those around her took notice.

After Sue's mother died, Aunt Janie raised Sue from a very young age. Aunt Janie taught Sue to cook, clean house, and do laundry. Many boys of color were taught gardening, janitorial work, and how to be chauffeurs. Aunt Janie, like a number minority individuals of her day, living in segregated cities, did not realize the potential of people of color. A lack of motivation and education sometimes led some to adopt a servile mentality.

Those were the days when a black person had to sit in segregated sections of movies, often the balconies. They were refused service in many restaurants. Churches were segregated. Even graveyards were segregated. Many inequities existed years ago in the United States, in the North as well as in southern states.

Anna went on to say, "yet in spite of circumstances and obstacles, African Americans changed their plight. Many did something about it and made a difference."

She went on to mention Booker T. Washington, the son of a slave who was born on a plantation. Washington later became an educator. In 1872, he attended Hampton Normal School (later, the Hampton Institute). Anna as an old woman had been an education major. She loved to remind people of the accomplishments of her people. She continued, "Later, old Booker T. became an instructor at Hampton and went on to become an organizer and principal of Tuskegee Normal School, which became Tuskegee Institute."

Jake Spencer, the journalist, patiently waited and listened as the aged Anna mentioned George Washington Carver, who was also born of slave parents in 1864. He worked his way through high school and graduated from the Iowa State College of Agriculture. He is remembered for the development of several hundred industrial uses of peanuts, sweet potatoes, and soybeans.

Her interviewer had to remind her that they were discussing Aunt Janie and Uncle Luke. She said, "But I did not tell you about Martin Luther King Jr., Rosa Parks, or Maya Angelou, who reminded us that 'No man can know where he is going unless he knows exactly where he has been.'"

The journalist smiled and asked again, "What about Aunt Janie and Uncle Luke?"

She then told him about Aunt Janie having a tongue sharper than a double-edged sword. She demanded respect and got it. Despite her religious beliefs, she often said a naughty word at times.

Uncle Luke was small of stature, quiet, and soft-spoken. His favorite biblical verse was Proverbs 13:18: "A soft answer turneth away wrath" (especially the wrath of Janie). He adored his wife and would come at her every beck and call.

Janie at times doted upon her little great niece, to the point of often forbidding the child's mother to chastise her own daughter. Once, Anna provoked her mother, who rushed toward the sassy child with intent to reprimand her for being naughty. Aunt Janie yelled, "Don't you touch that child!" Anna took refuge behind Aunt Janie (who failed to see the little angel stick out her tongue at her mother).

There were similar incidents Sue could not tolerate. She therefore moved away to the big city of Philadelphia, leaving her little daughter with her aunt and uncle. Aunt Janie would not permit Sue to take that child away.

Anna and Sandy were playmates and about one year apart in age. Sandy and her family lived in one of the luxury apartments above the janitor's quarters. Anna was invited to help celebrate birthdays with Sandy and her family. She also received lovely gifts from Sandy's parents. The two were inseparable. They played with dolls, coloring books, or sometimes just chased butterflies. There was a large grassy field in the center of the courtyard, surrounded by single homes. The two playmates had plenty of green grass upon which to run and play. They often put water in toy buckets and made mud pies and sand castles.

One day, after playing in the mud (and with dirty hands and faces to show for it), they decided to steal away across the field and make their way to a diner on their side of Lancaster Pike.

Those two grubby playmates entered the diner, sat on stools, and ordered ice-cream cones. When asked for money, they cheerfully replied that they had none. They were accommodated, if only to get those dirty little rascals out of the diner as quickly as possible. Customers displayed mixed emotions while observing the odd little couple.

Realizing that this was a way to get a daily treat, needless to say, these two continued to visit the diner, until one day the manager asked their names and phone numbers.

How thrilled they were to prove that they were smart enough to remember their phone numbers and even their addresses.

The manager, armed with that important information, visited their families and presented the parents with an ice-cream bill. He requested that they not return to the diner unescorted. Well, the impromptu trips to the diner ceased.

The old Anna said that the times spent with Aunt Janie and Sandy were extremely happy days. They lived in a quiet suburban area with plenty of room to run and play. People there seemed to love and accept her. She was extremely happy.

CHAPTER 2

One day, when Anna was seven years of age, her mother arrived to take Anna to the circus, which had pitched tents on a vacant lot near the suburban train station. The tents were within walking distance of Aunt Janie's residence. In anticipation, Anna kissed her great aunt and said, "Bye bye, I'll see you later, Aunty." Then she and her mother strolled along to the circus grounds. Anna was playfully skipping along and chattering while her mother gave the little one a smile as they continued along.

Upon reaching the circus grounds, the little one's eyes lit up. Multi-colored balloons were everywhere. There were booths selling cotton candy and ice cream. Anna observed the big tent, and imagined seeing acrobats, clowns, and tigers.

There was a very large tent featuring the main attractions in the middle of the lot, surrounded by smaller ones displaying supposed oddities of nature. A barker yelled "Step right up, folks … On the inside, for a small fee, you will see Jamee, half man and half woman! You'll also see a bearded lady, Siamese twins, the thinnest man on Earth, and many more."

Children at school talked about all of the exciting things they saw at the circus. Now, Anna would be able to tell of her experiences at the circus.

Years later, at another location, a circus would have a disastrous fire. Flames would ignite portions of the canvas tent and many people would be were injured. In years to come, many circuses would entertain men and women of all ages in sports stadiums, convention centers—or anywhere safer than a huge canvas tent.

As mother and child passed various stands, a man at a ticket booth shouted, "Step right up, folks! Get your tickets here. The show is about to start!" Anna grabbed her mother's arm and told her to hurry and get into the big tent before the show started.

It was then that Sue told her daughter that they would return to the circus another day, because they had a train to catch and did not want to miss it. "You are going home with me. We have to get on that train to the city before Aunt Janie sends someone looking for us."

Anna became extremely agitated and began to cry loudly as her mother continued to drag her along. Imagine the disappointment the young child was feeling at that time. Somehow, she felt deceived and lied to by someone she trusted. For days, she had anticipated going to the circus. It was a little child's dream. They waited about ten minutes for the train to arrive. Then the mother and her disappointed, teary-eyed youngster boarded the train and went off to the big city. Her mother never did take her to a circus.

Years later, as a young adult, Anna recalled that she worked for a family who owned a delicatessen at Tenth and Pike streets in Philadelphia. The circus pitched tents near her workplace. Circus employees ate at the deli. One of the hired hands arranged to have Anna enter the main tent via the employees' entrance. This fulfilled her latent desire to go to the circus.

As the train rolled along, Anna began to observe the scenery. They passed many green fields and country houses. Anna saw cows and horses in corrals. She curiously watched passengers board the train. Then she tried to read station signs when the train stopped to pick up and discharge passengers. The names of Bryn Mawr and Haverford gave her a bit of trouble. At one station she tried to speak the name on the sign: "Ard da more." Ever so slowly, and in broken syllables, she worked to understand it. Then, suddenly, she shouted "Ardmore!" so loudly that nearby passengers smiled. That game continued until she reached the big city.

They entered the city on Market Street. It was crowded and noisy. There were many people scurrying about. "Clang, clang, clang" went a big, ugly vehicle with poles on top. A pole dragged along a thick overhead wire, and sparked occasionally.

A frightened Anna took a firmer grip on her mother's hand. The strange sounds startled her. She had never seen a trolley. They boarded the trolley, where people sat on two long rows facing one another. A motorman drove while a conductor sat in the middle of the trolley in a small compartment. He collected fares as people passed him to either leave the trolley or sit in seats in the back. The vehicle rocked from side to side as it rolled along.

It turned off of Market Street onto Nineteenth and drove around Rittenhouse Square. Anna seemed pleased to see open space and people relaxing on park benches. She noticed birds and squirrels. She rode along, staring out of the windows, thinking that the city was really a nice place after all. Little did she realize that there were many facets to the big city. The trolley proceeded to travel around the square and onto South Nineteenth Street. They finally reached Christian Street, Sue's neighborhood.

There were people everywhere. There were huge three-story townhouses that were divided into at least five small apartments. In each house, there were two units on each floor (except the third floor, where there was only one small unit). On the third floor, tenants could walk out on to the roof of the rear second-floor apartment. Anna and her mother struggled to get around at least four or five people sitting on the front steps of the apartment building where Sue lived.

There were people resting on their elbows on pillows, their upper bodies extended out of windows. That was a method poor people used to get fresh air, as well as to socialize. "Hey Sue, is that your kid?" someone yelled. Sue responded, and another said something that Sue apparently did not understand. It probably was humorous, for it provoked a loud roar of laughter, which Sue ignored.

They maneuvered past the crowd of spectators and proceeded to enter a dimly lit hallway. Then they climbed up two flights of stairs to home. There, Anna observed one bedroom, a kitchen, and a small bathroom. There was a folding cot in the kitchen where Anna was to sleep.

From the kitchen window, she had a clear view of many back yards with tall wooden fences. Some of the yards were cluttered with debris. A dog was barking at a cat walking along the top of a fence. There were many pulley lines extending from the houses to poles in the back yards for drying clothes.

In her new home, Anna was bewildered. Looking around the room, she saw two front windows in the bedroom, overlooking the street. She saw a square-shaped Atwater Kent radio. There also was a child's rocking chair with a floral cushion in one corner of the room. "That is your chair," her mother told her. "Sit in it, try it out." It was quite comfortable. (That chair had a definite purpose, which will be explained later.)

"Oh, look what I have for my precious daughter!" her mother said. She opened a closet door and showed Anna new dresses and a few toys. The dresses were donated by a friend who worked in a dress factory. Learning of Sue's plot to get her daughter, the friend would slip a dress in her handbag under her worktable and take it home without ever paying for it. This was a common practice among many poor factory workers in the area.

"I have more dresses than this and lots of toys at home with Aunt Janie. I don't want these. I want to go home. I can't stay here!" Anna yelled. Then she began to scream and cry uncontrollably. Her mother grabbed her arm and knelt to the small child's level. She looked her straight in the eye and demanded, "Stop it! Stop it right now! This is your home now. If you do not stop it, I will definitely whip your butt."

That last statement brought Anna to the realization that she must obey. She said softly, "Aunt Janie won't like you if you hit me."

"Well, young lady," Sue replied, "Aunt Janie is not here now and you will do exactly as I say."

The situation was off to a bad start. Anna was used to being coddled by Aunt Janie, who loved her dearly

In Sue's neighborhood, many families with children were on welfare at that time. One criterion for being on welfare required that dependent children lived in the household with a parent. Because she did not have a steady job, Sue could qualify for subsistence, but only if her child lived with her. Some thought that was her reason for taking Anna. (This was a point open for speculation.)

Back in the suburbs, Aunt Jane placed her husband's dinner on the table. She decided that she would wait for Anna and her mother to return from the circus so the three of them could have dinner together. She anticipated seeing the joyous look on her great niece's face as she told her great aunt of all the things she had seen at the circus.

After a long wait, she became concerned because the two had not yet returned. "Luke, they left for the circus around 11:00. Why aren't they back yet? It is 7:30 in the evening. My intuition tells me that something is wrong.

My Lord, I wonder if my child is hurt. They could be in a hospital emergency room or something worse."

Her husband suggested that she call the hospital or the police if she was that worried. "Well, I don't need you to tell me what to do. Just help me to get to the phone so that I can call the hospital or the police. Hello, my name is Janie Anderson. Has there been an emergency involving a little girl and her mother? They went to the circus at 11:00 this morning and have not returned yet." The reply from the hospital was that there were no emergencies.

Next, she called the police. She was asked her relationship to the alleged missing persons. She was told that the child could not be reported missing if she was with her natural mother. "Do you have legal custody of that child?" she was asked. Receiving a negative reply, the officer said, "Then you cannot report your little niece missing, lady."

"Well, I damned sure will get legal custody," she said and terminated the conversation with a loud click.

CHAPTER 3

On her first night in her new home, Anna had just drifted off to sleep when someone opened the front door with a key and switched on the light in the bedroom. She heard a male voice with a deep resonance. This was strange to her. The last time she heard a similar voice was when she was sitting on Santa Claus's knee, telling him what she wanted for Christmas. What was he doing here in June, and why was he in her mother's apartment? She lay very still. Then she heard that thunderous voice ask, "Hey Sue, did you get the kid?"

"Yes, she is in the kitchen. Be quiet. Don't wake her up or she will start that crying again. I just cannot stand any more of that." Then the voices became inaudible.

A little later, she discerned the figure of a huge man walking into the kitchen in the dark. He looked like the ogre in one of her reading books. She dare not move, lest he notice that she was awake. Then he opened the door to the icebox and asked if Sue wanted a beer. She said yes, and he was asked again to lower his voice. He then returned to the bedroom. Traumatized by the events of the day, she eventually fell asleep for the second time.

"Wake up young lady and meet Mr. Jimmy." Her mother said as she approached her daughter's bed. "He came last night while you were sleeping. I want him to see my pretty little girl." Anna was thinking that she was not asleep and did not want to meet him either. However, she asked who he was, since she was anxious to know. Her mother told her that Mr. Jimmy was a friend. "You will see him quite often, so show him what a nice little lady you are."

When Anna was led into the room, she had a fearful look upon her face. Her countenance seemed to mirror her thoughts. Her mother chided her for looking so gloomy, so Anna forced a smile and faced the big guy. In a thunderous roar, she heard, "Well, hello, young lady. I have heard quite a bit about you."

Anna responded with a weak hello, and moved closer to her mother, who scolded her for being so bashful. The big man ordered the mother to be patient and let the kid get used to him. "Leave the kid alone and go fix breakfast."

Her mother did as commanded. Like Aunt Jane, he seemed to be protecting her. Gradually, Anna and the stranger managed to exchange a few words. He inquired about her schoolwork, and she asked where he lived. To her surprise, he revealed that he stayed there with her mother. Her next question would be to ask him why. However, this little six-year-old was intuitive enough not to rock the boat.

Later in the day, mother and daughter had a long talk about what she should do if she saw Aunt Janie riding around in her car. She and Uncle Luke owned a car, which neither of them drove. A friend chauffeured them around when needed.

Anna was to avoid being seen. When in the house, she was not to make a sound and by no means open the apartment door for anyone. "Those are my rules; obey them. Wondering why Aunt Janie would ever want to harm her, Annie simply uttered a quiet, "Yes, ma'am." A single tear trickled down her cheek.

Later that day, they had to go to the food store. They went down two flights of stairs. The hallway reeked of cooking odors. Many families lived in that building, which had been converted into a number of apartments. Each cook prepared something different, and the combined scents drifted out into the common hallway. The smell seemed a bit overwhelming, if not nauseating.

From one of the units, a female voice rang out. "Sue, is that you?" The mother answered her. Then the lady said, "I heard you got the kid." The door opened and she stood there dressed in a bathrobe, with rollers in her hair. Looking at Anna, she remarked how pretty the little one was. She then inquired about where the game would be on Saturday. Sue said it would be at her apartment. The lady said, "Okay, see you then," returned to her apartment, and closed the door.

The two resumed their trek to the grocery store. A huckster with a pushcart walked by. "Ice … coal!" he bellowed as he passed them and continued down the street still yelling, "Ice … coal!" Anna's mother explained that the man was selling ice for people's iceboxes from one section of his cart, and from the other, he sold bags of coal for those who lived in houses on the small streets who needed the coal in their small pot-belly stoves for heat.

Then came the banana man. His horse-drawn wagon was loaded with bananas. His pitch was "I Gotta Banan" which he said repeatedly as he rode along, stopping at intervals to sell bananas to the public. He was right out of the old country and had a deep Italian accent the children loved. Neighborhood children attempted to imitate him. No one said it like he did. He was charming.

In just one day, little Anna was aging far beyond her mere six years, with more surprises to come. She asked where all of the white people were, like Sandy and her family. She was in the ghetto and all she had seen so far were dark faces everywhere.

She had been living in the suburbs, where there were very few people who looked like her. Mother explained to her that many years ago, Africans who looked like her were captured in their homeland. They were placed in cages and put on slave ships that sailed to America. They were put on auction blocks and sold to rich white people to work in large fields in the South called plantations.

They had no freedom and worked long hours under the hot sun, picking cotton and tobacco. "Didn't Aunt Janie tell you these things?" the mother asked.

When the answer was no, Sue took time out. They sat on a nearby stone step while Sue decided that Anna must know something about her heritage.

"Some of those people worked in the slave owners' homes, cooking and cleaning or taking care of the owners' children. Many were beaten or killed for being disobedient. Sue said, "My great-grandfather and great-grandmother were once slaves. So, we are descendents of those Africans who once were taken from their land and sold to slave owners.

"Anna, there was a war called the Civil War. It was fought to free those unfortunate people. When the war ended, a president named Abraham Lincoln signed a bill called the Emancipation Proclamation that freed those people. Many of them traveled to New York, Detroit, and other northern cities, where they settled. Philadelphia is one of the cities where many freed slaves came to live.

"Those people had children, and their children gave birth to children, and now there are many people of color who look like us who live in areas like this. As our people moved into some of these northern cities, many whites moved away. There is another area in Philadelphia where people from Italy came to America and settled. They live in the Italian neighborhood." Sue promised to take her daughter to the Italian neighborhood one day and show her all of the fresh food markets. "The banana man lives in the Italian neighborhood," Sue explained. "Where many people who came from the same country live, that is called an ethnic neighborhood. There is a section in the city called Chinatown. There is an area where mostly people from Poland live, as well as other ethnic communities."

Sue may have been confusing her little daughter by telling her so much at one time about her heritage. She wondered if Anna understood what she was being told. Little Anna asked, "Did Sandy and her mom and dad have slaves and beat them?" "No, Anna. Those things happened many years ago. People who did those terrible things are not alive now. Sandy's family is not responsible for all of the bad things that happened to people of color long ago. Sandy and her mother and father are very nice, loving people. You know that."

To comply with her daughter's inquiry concerning the absence of white people in their area, the mother said, "Come on, young lady. I will introduce you to some very nice people." They arose from the steps where they were sitting, and went around the corner to the food store, which was owned by a very nice Jewish family.

There, Anna met Mrs. Schwartz, who knew Sue and called her by name. She was surprised to know that Sue had a little daughter. She made a remark about how attractive the little girl was and that mother and daughter had similar features. This pleased the two of them.

When it came time to pay for the items purchased, the store owner produced a notebook from beneath the counter and recorded the amount spent. Sue took out her little book and compared notes. This was the method poor people used to pay for their food in those days. The grocery bills were paid when the customers received their checks.

On the way from the grocery store, they met many people who lived in the neighborhood. Most of them knew Sue. She stopped to chat and to acquaint them with Anna. Then they headed back to Christian Street and to Anna's new home.

One day, Sue was busy cleaning her small apartment. She emptied trash and picked up loose articles that were scattered around. She also fried chicken and made potato salad. Anna was bathed and dressed. When she asked the reason for all of the preparation, Anna was told that it was game night.

Excitedly, Anna wanted to know if she was going to play games.

"No," her mother explained. "Some of my friends will be over to play pinochle. It is something we adults do on Friday nights. You can play with your toys and keep busy until you get sleepy, and rest in my bed until the company leaves."

This did not seem like fun to Anna, who simply acquiesced, which was her way of coping with difficult situations.

Mr. Jimmy arrived with a package and Sue called out, "Did you get the stuff?" He addressed her as "woman" and told her not to ask silly questions. Hearing that, Anna wondered what the "stuff" could be. She dared not ask because once, when she interrupted an adult conversation, she was told that children should be seen and not heard.

Evening came and so did the players. Two couples who lived in the building arrived almost simultaneously.

They were loud and boisterous. Fortunately for Anna, one couple had an eight-year-old daughter, Edna, with them. The two young ones immediately became friends. They played with Anna's few toys and colored in her crayon books. At times, they seem to giggle a lot. Anna was having fun and enjoyed playing with Edna.

The last two couples came, announcing their arrival rather loudly while ascending the stairway. Two couples sat at the kitchen table and played cards while the third couple waited to play the winners of that game. They laughed constantly and playfully called one another names, occasionally uttering a few obscene expressions.

They played a game of "drink or smell." The couple that won the game of pinochle would get to take a drink of whiskey. The loser had to smell it. There was much teasing and laughter going on.

In the meantime, the children enjoyed their time together. While playing, Edna revealed a few secrets concerning what transpired in her parents' chamber when the lights go out at night. Then there was a flurry of mischievous laughter. Edna advised Anna to pretend to be asleep at night and listen to the strange sounds coming from the other side of the bedroom door. Little Anna was learning about adult behavior at the ripe old age of six. Sue's elders had an expression, "Every shut eye ain't sleep." So very true.

Anna was now experiencing life in the ghetto. Living among the affluent was not ideal for a little girl of color in those days. Anna always remembered how fortunate she was to have experienced a better way of life. The environment her mother chose for her was depressing. She missed being in the wide-open fields and chasing butterflies. She missed her friend Sandy. And she missed Aunt Janie most of all.

Neighbors met in one another's apartment on a regular basis. Often, it would be game night. Other times, someone would throw a rent party in order to raise enough money to pay the rent for that month. They sold dinners and pitchers of beer and shots of whiskey in their apartments. Many times, they sold untaxed bootleg corn liquor. However, all of that was illegal.

Once, when Sue threw her rent party, a jealous neighbor alerted the police, who drove around in red patrol cars. A lookout spotted the police patrol car with blinking lights as it turned the corner. "The red car is coming. Hide the booze!" he said to the partygoers. The corn whiskey was in small, flat flasks that could be concealed easily.

Mr. Jimmy quickly passed the containers to Sue, who placed them under the cushion of Anna's rocking chair. She told Anna to sit there and not move. "The police will not hurt you. You can smile at them if you want, but do not get up or say anything."

Soon, police were running up the stairs to the third floor. They yelled, "Police! Open the door or we will break it in." Mr. Jimmy let them in and explained that they were entertaining friends. Little Anna rocked back and forth in her in her little chair, not uttering a word.

"Are you folks selling booze in here? Okay, where's the corn liquor? We know it is in here." Everyone remained calm as the police searched women's handbags, men's pockets, bureau drawers, under the beds, the icebox, and even went out on the roof over the second-floor apartment. They found nothing. One of them remarked how cute the little girl with that sweet smile was.

They searched for about a half hour before deciding that there was no illegal whiskey in the apartment. They left empty-handed. Descending the stairway, one said that the snitch lied to them and they gave him money. "In a tiny place like that, there is no way in hell they could hide that corn liquor without our finding it," one said as they departed.

A crowd gathered outside, hoping to see someone get arrested. They were disappointed when the police left without arresting anyone. On the third floor, everyone laughed and bragged about how little Anna sat there rocking and smiling. She helped fool the policemen and became a heroine that evening.

CHAPTER 4

Meanwhile, life on Christian Street went rather uneventfully. Mother worked as a day worker who cleaned houses in the northeast section of the city two or three days each week. During her absence, Anna was told remain inside and not answer the door. They had no telephone. Neighborhood residents used an outdoor payphone on the corner.

Occasionally, when her mother was at home, Anna was allowed to play outside with the children. She learned to play all of the games inner-city kids played in that era. They played double-Dutch jumping rope, hopscotch, I spy, and a hide-and-seek game called red light.

The aged Anna continued to recall the day that she was looking out the front window and she spotted Aunt

Janie's car. The driver was slowly cruising along, asking children questions. Her mother was at home at the time. Sue and Anna stood back and watched. Sue had given her aunt the general location where she lived, but not the exact address.

"That lady just won't quit," she muttered quietly. Anna asked why she could not go down there and see Aunt Janie. She was told that her mother would explain that fact to her later.

When the car was first spotted, it was on the opposite side of the street. Then it moved on to their side. It neared their residence. A neighbor's child, being questioned, pointed to the third floor where Sue and Anna lived. "Oh my God …" Sue murmured. "She found us. Quick, get out of sight."

The great aunt was unable to climb the stairs. It was a big effort just to get into her vehicle. Frank, the driver, entered the building. Soon he was knocking on their door and calling Sue and Anna. He knocked several times while mother and daughter stood motionless. "If you are in there, listen to me. We know where you live now. I suggest that you call your aunt Janie. There will be big trouble if you don't get in touch with her." Then he descended the stairs and spoke briefly to Aunt Janie, who sat in the back seat of the automobile. Then they departed.

The atmosphere became extremely tense for a few months, with no further incidents. Sue began to relax.

Her aunt was leaving her alone. Maybe she had just given up.

One day, on her way to the grocery store, someone called Sue by name. Instinctively, she answered. A strange man told her that he had something for her and handed her a summons to appear in court. "Just what is that lady up to now?" she said. "What right does she have to do this?" Sue was the child's natural mother and had not given the child up for adoption, as her aunt requested a number of times.

Sue never relinquished her rights or granted legal guardianship to her aunt. The woman was old and could not move around fast enough to keep up with a six-year-old. She had to appear in court. As requested, Sue went to court. Aunt Janie was there with Uncle Luke and Frank, the driver. She had a lawyer.

When Sue's case was called, little Anna was removed from the courtroom and placed in a large room with many books and toys. What transpired at that trial was not known to Anna. She recalled seeing her mother leave the courtroom in tears. She had to turn her daughter over to the aunt that day. Sobbing, Sue hugged and kissed little Anna, saying, "That wasn't fair, the terrible things they said about me in there." Anna went home with her great aunt, and Sue went home alone.

Chapter 5

The year following the court case seemed to pass quickly. Back in the small suburban town, Anna and Sandy enjoyed playing together again. She returned to school. Anna did well. Her mother visited a number of times. The judge ordered supervised visits, for fear of another circus incident being repeated.

Back on Christian Street, Sue's neighbors asked many questions. A few showed empathy toward her and criticized the aunt. They queried the wisdom of a child being taken away from her birth mother and given to an old lady. Others merely said money talks and that the old lady was better off financially to care for the little girl. Sue, was extremely knowledgeable of the reason and never revealed to anyone the accusations made against her. After her daughter became of age, Sue still kept that secret to herself.

One day in September, Frank the driver came again to the door, saying that he had an extremely important message for Sue. Realizing that he was sincere, she let him in. He had bad news that her aunt was extremely ill and bedridden. Sue was needed to help with her aunt's care. Without hesitation, she placed the ugly courtroom scene behind her and prepared to leave as soon as possible.

Back at her aunt's home, a close friend of the family answered the door. The friend explained Aunt Janie's condition. She had dropsy, a serious accumulation of fluids in the cavities or tissues in her body. It could slowly progress to the point of possibly being a terminal illness.

The friend had done all that she could to help. Now she had to return to her home to see about her family. Sue was needed to care for her daughter and her aunt.

Sue thanked the friend and went into her aunt's room. When she entered the room, she saw a very sick old woman propped up by a number of pillows. Her breathing was labored. She turned her head toward the door when she heard it open. Looking up and seeing Sue standing there, she said slowly, "I must be really sick for them to send for you."

After a brief moment of silence, Sue leaned over and kissed her aunt on the cheek.

She told her aunt that she loved her and appreciated everything her aunt had done for her and little Anna. "Please don't talk too much. I know that is very hard for you to do," Sue said. They both smiled at that remark, for it certainly was true. "Conserve your energy so that you can get better." Janie was unable to move unassisted. Someone had to take care of her every personal need.

Sue stayed and gave her aunt a great degree of loving care. It must have been difficult for such a strong, self-reliant person like Janie to lie helplessly dependent upon others for her every need. Sue arranged for a minister to pray with her aunt and to give her the Holy Communion sacrament.

The doctor informed them that Aunt Janie's vital signs were failing. Her condition was regressing to a point that soon she would lapse into a coma, followed by death. At times, little Anna entered her aunt Janie's room and kissed her. She tried to get Aunt Janie to talk to her. Often there was only a one-word response or a faint smile of recognition.

Before Janie lapsed into a coma, she did utter three words: "I'm so tired." The next day, her spirit departed from her ailing body. When her great aunt died, Anna was confined to her room with the door closed until after the body was removed. The morticians and assistants arrived and prepared her body for removal. They slowly wheeled the corpse down the long, narrow corridor to the front door. They seemed to be struggling profusely, for little Anna could hear wheels screeching and voices giving directions outside of her door.

When Anna was allowed to leave her room she asked many questions. She was told that Aunt Janie had to go away and people were helping her to leave. "Where did she go?" Anna asked. She was told that her great aunt had gone to be with the Lord and would not be coming back. This prompted a volley of inquiries. Her mother told her that they would explain everything to Anna later. That was the answer older people gave children in those days. Usually, that was the final answer.

CHAPTER 6

The clock appeared to be running backward for Anna. After the funeral, she returned to Christian Street with her mother. She cried a lot and often wondered why Aunt Janie left her to be with the Lord before she had a chance to grow up. She was very happy with her great aunt. Her young life began with disappointments. Her dad left, Aunt Janie went to be with the Lord, and Mr. Jimmy was not coming around anymore. At least he seemed to take up for her at times. Now even he was gone. She felt deserted.

Next, her mother hired a man to move their meager belongings in a pushcart from the apartment on the third floor to another two-room apartment on the second floor two blocks away on Christian Street, where two families shared the bathroom. The other family did not always clean the tub after a bath, and the toilet—well, that was another story. They also had problems with household pests..

There was some doubt in her mind concerning the love that her mother had for her. Her mother was beginning to show little or no affection toward her, and she stayed out very late at night, leaving Anna alone. She felt emotionally abandoned.

The feeling of not being loved or being in the way can become instilled in a child's mind. That feeling never entirely went away in Anna's mind. It lasted throughout her teenage years and even into adulthood.

Sue's mother was not in her childhood life. Sue had two stepmothers. They and her father showed no affection for her. They were strict disciplinarians. Then Aunt Janie took over. Those two were forever in one conflict after another. As an adult, it appeared that Sue was forever looking for love and affection from each of her male friends, who deceived or abandoned her. Both Sue and her daughter had serious emotional and psychological problems.

Little Anna's mother left her alone in a small apartment, often until well past midnight. She could hear voices in the hallway and feared that someone would break into their apartment and harm her. She lay tense and afraid, unable to sleep until after her mother returned home.

She was enrolled in a school one block away from where she lived on Christian Street. Classroom work came easy for her because of her early schooling in the suburban school. She had a slight advantage scholastically over the inner-city schoolchildren her age. Her school on Christian Street was issued used textbooks, some with soiled or missing pages.

Often when she raised her hand to answer a question, the teacher would call on someone else, sometimes saying, "Anna, you know the answer. Give someone else a chance to respond." This made her unpopular with her fellow students.

Fights would occur after school. When crowds of children assembled to watch a fight, Anna would rush home to avoid being involved or being beaten. She wore a door key around her neck to enter her apartment, because her mother was never home when she returned from school. (She, like many others, were called "latchkey kids" in those days.)

One day, Anna was unable to reach home before being approached by classroom bullies. They taunted her and called her Miss Smarty and Teacher's Pet. When she raised her hand to avoid being hit, one of them yelled, "Oh, so you want to fight?"

Anna received a number of hard hits before a passerby halted the altercation, which pleased her immensely. She went home alone and cried again.

Philadelphia schools were integrated back in the 1930's. However, children were assigned to a school in their district. This was a type of "de facto" segregation, resulting in those resided in a basically segregated neighborhood, must attend a basically segregated school. Better-qualified teachers preferred to teach in more affluent areas of town. This left some children who were slow learners at a disadvantage.

Despite the quality of certain schools, many African-American children from the poorest neighborhoods succeeded. Some became teachers, social workers, doctors, lawyers, scientists, college professors, journalists, and many more. Years later, in Anna's neighborhood, a young black man was hired on the editorial staff of one of Philadelphia's leading newspapers.

Also during Anna's time in Philadelphia, there was a black city controller hired who was reared in her same disadvantaged area. With focus and determination, one can beat the odds.

Old Anna in the senior home predicted that one day, the United States of America could have an African-American president in the White House. Maya Angelou said, "And Yet I Rise."

Many fine, upstanding, hard-working, blue-collar workers, electricians, plumbers, carpenters, sanitation department employees, and many other citizens are successful individuals. They are to be lauded for their achievements.

In any goal people choose, if they are good at what they do, they can be successful in life. People should aim to be the best at whatever they do.

One day, Sue introduced Anna to an attractive young man. He was short of stature and spoke with an accent. The new suitor's name was Manuel. Soon, he and Anna's mother shared an apartment together. He was friendly to Anna and treated her with respect, except for one minor incident, in which Anna could not understand the motive for his actions.

Anna had a habit of sleeping with her favorite doll baby with her in her bed. When she was younger, it was her teddy bear that she cuddled until she drifted off to sleep.

Manuel entered the room in which she was sleeping one evening and almost threw a tantrum. Young Anna was snuggling under her covers, endearingly embracing her doll baby. "Take that baby out of your bed and don't you ever let me see you in bed with a baby again!" he said with raised voice. Anna began to cry.

Sue rushed into the room and questioned Manuel about what is so wrong with Anna taking her doll to bed with her. He explained that in his country, girls do not do that. To him, it appeared that she wanted to have a baby and that she lay there like an unwed mother nestling her baby. She had plenty of time to grow up, get married, and have her own real baby in bed with her.

Sue said, "That sounds silly to me. Leave the child alone. That is utterly ridiculous. What kind of country is that? What is wrong with her sleeping with her doll? It's only a toy." Manuel's face was flushed. He stood there for a brief moment and said, "As long as you want me around, doll sleeps here." He tossed the doll in the toy box. "Anna sleeps here," he said, and pointed to Anna's bed. "No doll baby in your bed, young lady."

To Sue, the entire episode was much ado about nothing. Anna was sobbing. Her mother was angry. Manuel defiantly made a decision that it was his way or no way. Sue acquiesced. She needed Manuel in her life at that time. Anna was not to sleep with her favorite doll anymore.

Manuel announced that he and Sue were getting married. Anna was to have a new dad. They moved to an apartment on South Nineteenth Street. The moving man with his pushcart was summoned again. On one corner was a grocery store called the American Store. The exterior was painted yellow. On the inside, sawdust was on the floor. There were large pickle barrels on the floor. Across from the apartment was a small family-owned grocery store.

Children often played in a small street directly across from the apartment where they lived. In the middle of that street, they played a game. It was called Dead Block, and squares were marked off in the street. The game was played with a checker that was projected with the fingers from one block to the other. Old Anna forgot the object of the game, but said it was fun. They also played half ball, which was a game of baseball played with a rubber ball cut in half, so that it would not break any windows or hurt someone.

Children played hopscotch. One of the girls' favorite games was jacks; they played on neighbors' marble steps, which they scrubbed weekly to keep them white. One favorite game for girls in the city was jump rope or double Dutch.

Anna soon found that South Philly streets were not all alike. Many very nice people lived in South Philadelphia. Some lived in single-family homes and maintained their areas with pride. They occasionally hosed down small streets and pavements. Many had planters outside of their homes. On special occasions, residents obtained permits to close off their block and have block parties with music and home-cooked food.

A large gray stone church stood on the corner of Nineteenth and Catherine streets, where neighborhood children were invited to attend Sunday school. Anna and some of her friends enjoyed being there on Sunday mornings. They loved singing songs and reading about Jesus and His love for little children.

They were getting religious training for the very first time since Aunt Janie went to be with the Lord. The children went to school together, and life was good for her. Anna was completely happy living in South Philadelphia.

CHAPTER 7

Less than six months had passed, when Manuel announced that he had rented a house in Camden, New Jersey for his wife and stepdaughter. It was moving time again. This, as Anna recalled, was move number four. (Or was it number five?) And now, she was only eight years old. Just as she settled in her new surroundings, it was time to move again. It was crying time again. This move was devastating for her. It was "bye-bye, happiness."

Moving day came amid tears and sad goodbyes. The pushcart man was not needed this time, because Manuel purchased furnishings in New Jersey. The family moved into a two-bedroom townhouse on Lawrence Street in Camden.

Manuel worked at the Walt Whitman Hotel near city hall. It catered to upscale clientele. The hotel was named after the poet who in 1855 published the book, "Leaves of Grass." It contained twelve untitled poems written in long cadence lines like the unrhymed verse of the King James Bible *(Wagnall's Encyclopedia)*.

Later, the Walt Whitman Bridge connecting South Jersey with South Philadelphia was constructed.

Lawrence Street appeared to be a satisfactory move for little Anna. Their house was comfortable and assuredly a step up from the apartments in which they had been living. Anna had her own big bedroom and place for all her toys. Going to the very large bathroom, one had to pass through Anna's bedroom. It appeared that the bathroom was an added convenience and may have been a third bedroom at one time. When the house was constructed, it probably had an outdoor toilet in the back yard. They were pleased that the bathroom was in the house.

Manuel had friends who lived across the street. They had four children with whom Anna played. She encountered one fight in her new neighborhood. While playing with a group of children on a vacant lot down the street from her home, someone suggested playing prize fighting in an abandoned truck body that resembled a boxing ring.

Anna was chosen to be one of the boxers. Fearing embarrassment and future teasing, she complied and climbed into the bed of the truck. The contenders went to their respective corners. Someone yelled, "Ding-Ding, Round One!" The challengers came out of their corners. At first, Anna took a painful beating. The pounding caused a stinging sensation to her face and upper body. How relieved she was to hear, "Ding-Ding, Round one is over!"

By the time round two began, Anna knew that she had to follow through. She returned to the ring with every intent of winning. She was a scared fighter. Her fists were flailing non-stop. Feeling no pain now, she defended her honor. By then, the other kids could see that Anna was becoming victorious. A voice rang out, "Ding- Ding, Fight's over. It's a draw." In times of stress, one part of the adrenal gland secretes an excessive amount of adrenaline. During her harrowing ordeal, Anna's adrenaline level had to have ascended sky high.

She was enrolled in an elementary school not far from where they lived. The aged Anna attempted to recall the name of the school. She thought it was Powell Elementary.

During the summer months, a few teenagers accompanied some of the smaller children to a swimming pool in South Camden. It was about a forty-five-minute walk, one way. That was the only pool in the area that accommodated people of color at that time. With swimsuits under their shorts and towels around their necks, they happily trudged along to the swimming pool and had a wonderful time.

On Sundays, many in the community dressed in their Sunday best to attend church. Women wore hats and white gloves. They took pride in dressing up. It was a tradition. They attended a small church nearby. Years later, that block of Lawrence Street was apparently taken by eminent domain to expand the access to the Delaware River Bridge between North Camden and Center City, Philadelphia.

Some evenings, Sue and a few of the neighbors played pinochle at different homes. Passersby could hear the laughter from within when nearing a home where the game was being played. Anna could always locate her mother, wherever she was playing, because Sue's voice rang out louder than the rest. Anna was beginning to like living in New Jersey.

CHAPTER 8

Soon after Anna's ninth birthday, she overheard Manuel and Sue discussing an impending trip to Washington, D.C. Unable to decipher their entire conversation, she assumed that the three of them were to take a vacation to D.C. Much to her dismay, she was to stay with Manuel's friend across the street while Manuel and Sue went away.

They were away four days and returned, announcing the good news that the family was moving to Washington. Anna would be able to see the Capitol Building, the Washington Monument, and the White House where the president of the United States lived.

They expected Anna to be happy with the news. But it was not so. She would be leaving friends again. All she felt was despair. She was unable to share their joyous feelings.

There was a jazz singer named Ella Fitzgerald who recorded the song that featured the lyrics, "Into each life, some rain must fall, but too much is falling in mine." That could have been Anna's theme song.

The family told friends and neighbors of their plans. Many moments of sadness followed. Their short stay in New Jersey was coming to an end. Manuel and Sue began hastily packing personal belongings. They would be staying temporarily with relatives, so they would place household furnishing in storage until they found a house in D.C.

Many of Anna's favorite toys were placed in storage. She remembered that the stored items were subsequently lost in storage due to non-payment of the storage fees.

Relatives who had a modest home on Lane Place met them. They lived near Kenilworth Avenue in northeast Washington D.C. Anna shared a room with her cousin Beth. The aunt with whom they were living had a garden on a vacant lot across the street from her home. They worked in the garden at times, pulling up weeds or collecting vegetables. Neighborhood kids used to steal watermelons from the garden.

They had a dog named Butch who would chase anyone in uniform. They had to keep him in the house when the mailman was delivering in the area.

Once Butch threatened a policeman on a motorcycle at a corner near their home. The officer drew his gun. Anna and Beth ran, screaming, "Please don't shoot him. Please, we will take him home!" The policeman said, "You had better get him pretty damned quick or he will be a dead dog." They managed to rescue Butch that day.

Across the railroad tracks from where they lived was the town of Deanwood where people congregated on weekends. There were swings for the children. People carried picnic baskets and watched Negro baseball teams play. Anna recalled black baseball players were not allowed to play with Major League teams. A number of great black baseball players had their start playing sandlot baseball in towns like Deanwood.

Segregation existed in most areas of the city at that time. It was extremely visible in residential neighborhoods, restaurants, department store employees, etc. Public transportation in the city of Washington was not segregated at that time (around 1936). However, leaving Washington going south, all buses and trains were segregated.

Sue and Beth's mother, Aunt Phyllis, played the numbers game daily. A numbers man would come to the house and collect the bets, which he called in to his employer. Each bet consisted of three digits, similar to the lottery games played by the states. The old untaxed numbers game was illegal. The states later began the lottery and taxed the winnings. The numbers man in the old days secretly made his rounds daily. If caught in his activity, he would have been arrested by the police. The winning numbers were selected by listening to the daily horse races at various racetracks. The results of the first three races could be heard each weekday on radio broadcasts.

These facts, Anna seemed to recall, happened in her day. That was a favorite pastime for people in some neighborhoods. The price of playing a three-digit number could be as little as one or two cents. Aunt Phyllis played as many as fifty or sixty numbers on a daily basis, often winning small sums of money for her efforts. They could play leads. After the first two digits of a number were revealed, they could bet on the third number. This was great for players, because the odds were then only ten to one.

Local stores sold dream books, which interpreted the meanings of dreams. Those books also suggested lucky numbers for different dreams. It was amazing to note the various ways people devised to play the illegal numbers game back in the 1930s (and a number of years beyond).

Aunt Phyllis also cared for neighborhood children of working mothers. Her income seemed to be adequate, despite the fact that she was a widow with no other means of support.

While living in Washington, Anna saw a postcard from her father that had been forwarded to her mother. Her father tried to locate his family through a relative in Philadelphia, who forwarded a card to Sue in Washington. Anna tried to memorize the address. She sent a letter to him that was returned marked undeliverable. Sue wanted no contact with Anna's dad because she had married again without benefit of a divorce. Manuel was unaware of that fact until much later, when he decided to remarry.

Sue said that she had misplaced that card. Anna regretted not being able to get in touch with her father. Manuel was not told about the correspondence from the first husband. Soon thereafter, for some undisclosed reason, the family returned to Philadelphia.

CHAPTER 9

Their next home was in West Philadelphia with Sue's father and her stepmother, whom the children called Grammom. Anna shared a room with three girls. Manuel and Sue had a room, and a young married couple rented a bedroom next to the one bathroom in the house.

Late at night, the two oldest girls would sneak a peek at Papa Joe's buttocks as he ambled down the long hall to the bathroom. He wore long underwear with a split down the middle in the back. He walked with a limp. The split would open and close with the rhythm of his gait. The girls would stick their heads out of the bedroom door as soon as he passed and were silently amused at seeing his black rump appear and disappear behind that flap in his long johns.

Once, they could not contain their giggling; their heads bounced back into their room to avoid detection. This brought a verbal scolding with the threat of a spanking if they did not stop that noise and go to sleep.

Another mischievous thing the two older girls did was to go into the bathroom late at night and put an ear to the wall adjoining the married couple's room to listen to their lovemaking.

One night, Manuel caught those two in the bathroom together. They had a good bit of explaining to do. That ended their surveillance.

Flo was the oldest. Then there was Mae and Amy. Flo and Anna often quarreled. While making up beds one day, Anna pulled a sheet away from Flo, who snatched it back. Angry words followed. This precipitated a vigorous tug-of-war between the two. They began to fight. Sue remembered that she had been physically challenged when she was younger living in New Jersey when children played a boxing ring game. She did well then.

This time, she retaliated with the confidence of David against Goliath. The fight continued across the bed and onto the floor. They fought from the bedroom into the hallway, rolling over and hitting one another. The youngest, Amy, witnessed the ordeal. She yelled, "Grammom! They're fighting!"

She was screaming when Grammom came running up the stairs. She had a difficult time separating the two warriors. They landed powerful blows upon one another. Both were crying as they were pulled apart. Anna recalled that she thought the referee may have received a blow during that altercation. From that point on, those two adversaries had the utmost respect for one another and became best buddies.

Anna remembered there were two double beds in Papa Joe and Grammom's room. Once, while the grandmother was in the basement washing clothes, Anna and one of the girls decided to jump from one bed to the other. They made trampolines out of the beds. They were jumping back and forth, really enjoying their new play equipment. Suddenly an angry grandmother burst into the room with strap in hand.

"You are going to ruin my beds. Don't ever do that again." She began whacking behinds and legs. The two girls were crying and yelling with screeches that could wake the dead. Their bodies and legs were stinging in pain. The enforcer left the room, leaving the sobbing girls to compare the welts that began to appear.

As Jake Spencer, the journalist, was interviewing Anna, she admitted that corporal punishment was brutal. She whipped her children when they were young because she was whipped as a child. She thought that was the way to discipline children. If she could turn back the clock, she would have found better ways to reprimand her children.

The King James Bible, Proverbs 23:13 states, "Withhold not correction from the child. For if thou beatest him with the rod, he shall not die. Proverbs 23:14 states, Thou shall beat him with the rod and shalt deliver him from hell." Papa Joe not only would attempt to deliver the child from hell—he tried to beat the hell out of the child. He often said, "Spare the rod, spoil the child."

Anna said many families in following generations considered corporal punishment a form of child abuse. A child should respect his parents, not fear them. Withholding privileges or taking away that favorite toy should be just as effective and less brutal.

CHAPTER 10

There was a car barn in the next block where trolley cars were housed. Out-of-service trolleys received maintenance by mechanics who worked in trenches below the tracks. That area was off limits to the public. Children often ran through the building and were chased out by employees. Anna sometimes ran through there with other children.

The old trolley cars were powered by long poles with connectors that rolled along overhead wires. Many could be operated from the front and the back. They had two power poles. At the end of their route, they could be switched from one track to the other and return to their starting point.

Each morning, Anna remembered hearing screeching metal-on-metal sounds as trolley wheels scoured against tracks while turning out of the car barn onto the street. They made an annoying, high-pitched, harsh sound that awakened Anna as she lay in bed very early in the mornings.

The milkmen delivered milk in glass bottles to people's homes. They drove horse-drawn wagons. They later replaced metal wheels with rubber tires, which resulted in a quieter ride. The sounds of horses' hooves were somewhat annoying early in the mornings. Anna said that hoof beats of their feet made a sound that went "clippity clop." The horses seemed to know the route. As the driver delivered milk to one house, the horse proceeded to the next one and stopped. That was very interesting.

During extremely cold weather in Philadelphia, milk left on doorsteps would freeze. The frozen cream would rise to the top of the glass bottle and extend a few inches above. That was a perfect example of the expression, "Cream rises to the top." Years later, the process of homogenization divided fat particles in milk so that the cream could no longer separate under those circumstances.

There was a young man in the neighborhood studying to be an accomplished pianist. He practiced daily for hours, filling the air with the most melodious sounds. Those who never heard of Mozart, Bach, Beethoven, Tchaikovsky and others were being introduced to music that many paid high prices to enjoy at the Academy of Music.

The sound of hucksters, the iceman, and men selling fruits and vegetables were sounds Anna remembered hearing. They drove horse-drawn wagons, each emitting a sound unique to his trade. Before street sweepers would clean up behind the horses, some housewives would collect the horse manure to put into their flowerpots. Their plants grew big and beautiful.

The first time Anna remembered hearing the religious song "Just a Closer Walk with Thee" was when she saw a man was walking along the street singing. He was not very well dressed. He had a beautiful tenor voice and carried a collection of tracts containing the words to that song. He would stop and pass out the words to anyone who would give him a small donation.

He delivered many tracts that day and was amply compensated. His voice faded away as he continued singing, "I am weak, but thou art strong. Jesus, keep me from all wrong. I'll be satisfied at long as I walk, let me walk close to thee."

There was an amusing sound that lingered in Anna's mind. Grammom provided dinner for an elderly man, Mr. Bill, who rented a room next door to them. Everyone ate dinner together. He had loose-fitting false teeth. He chewed his food with an annoying clicking sound that amused the children. They often gave sly glances to one another and giggled. Papa Joe scolded them when he noticed what they were doing.

One day, the oldest girl clicked her teeth with her fork, making a sound similar to the boarder's loose-fitting teeth. All four girls burst out in a fit of laughter. Upon noticing how amused the girls were, he began to laugh with them. He did not realize that they were making fun of him. Upon seeing him so amused, all of the girls became hysterical and were sent from the table to their rooms.

They were verbally admonished later, but received no corporal punishment. Papa Joe and Grammom may have been a bit amused as well at the sight of Mr. Bill laughing and not realizing the girls were mimicking him.

CHAPTER 11

A classmate at school told Anna that her mother rooted a sweet potato in water and grew a lovely climbing vine. Anna realized that Grammom would never allow her to play with food they needed to eat, so she selected a convenient time when her grandmother was preoccupied, and obtained a sweet potato from the pantry for her botanical experiment. She placed the tuber in a jar of water and searched for a place to hide it. Hearing someone approaching, she quickly hid it in the back of a hallway closet beneath the first-floor stairway.

So much clutter had accumulated there that the jar was completely out of sight. At times, when no one was around, she would add more water. Long roots sprouted from the bottom, and there seemed to be some activity on the top. Anna was very pleased with its progress.

Eventually, she forgot about her little experiment. Leaves sprouted on top and thick roots filled the bottom of the jar. Then the water dried out. All that was left was a moldy jar with dried leaves and roots.

Spring arrived and Grammom decided to give the hall closet a thorough cleaning. On her knees, she slowly pulled out objects. As she worked her way toward the back of the closet, she spotted the moldy jar filled with dried leaves and roots.

She began to yell, "Oh my Lord! Oh my Lord!" The girls came running to find out what had upset her. "Somebody is working voodoo on me!" she cried. "Look at those roots back in the corner. Somebody put a spell on me!" The girls had never seen her so frightened. She was crying and walking around in circles. "Oh my Lord, Oh my Lord!" Anna knew it was her potato, but she was too scared to admit it then.

Apparently, Grammom believed that the appearance of roots in her home was an indication that someone had cast a spell on her. She was in an extreme state of panic. She called her friends, who decided that she needed a medium to conduct a meeting at her home. That person could supposedly summon spirits of dead relatives who would protect her from evil spirits with intent to harm her.

The night of that important meeting, the children were told to stay in their room with the door closed. Papa Joe went to bed, early as usual, stating that he had no time for that foolishness. He said that she should get on her knees and ask God to protect her. The older girls lay silently at the top of the stairway, anxiously waiting to hear what was going on.

The spiritualist arrived, dressed in black. Lights were extinguished and candles were lit. Then someone closed the living room door. From the room came humming and chanting. "Are you there? I feel your presence," the spiritualist's voice rang out several times.

The girls at the top of the stairway rushed back into their room and pulled covers over their heads. The spirits summoned would know they were at the top of the stairs.

Spirits of dead relatives apparently shielded Grammom from the evil spirits, for the next morning she felt confident enough to remove those roots from her closet and burn them in the coal furnace in the basement. From that point on, she went about her chores, singing hymns and praising the Lord. The spell had been lifted.

Chapter 12

Life went along smoothly for about three years until one day Sue announced that she was leaving Manuel. She decided that the marriage was a mistake. Manuel was a nice man, but West Philadelphia was boring—and so was Manuel.

Soon she moved away and returned to South Philadelphia, leaving her daughter and her husband with her father and his second wife. She rarely visited her daughter. Sue was living a carefree lifestyle amid friends with whom she had something in common. She occasionally visited a church in her area. She joined the Elks Club and their marching band.

A few relatives maliciously implied that she lived a life of party-going, drinking, and possibly promiscuity.

Overhearing character assassinations about her mother deeply distressed Anna.

Manuel was well liked by everyone. He eventually fell in love with a neighbor. After a brief courtship, they married and purchased a home nearby. The couple visited Grammom often and chatted about many subjects, some of which included Sue. The new marriage was successful and they lived harmoniously until Manuel died many years later.

One Christmas, after Sue had abandoned Manuel and her daughter, all of the girls received gift boxes not to be opened until Christmas. The three older girls received gifts of clothing. The youngest had clothing and toys. On Christmas morning, they all rushed downstairs to open their gift boxes. When Anna opened hers, she found to her dismay that the dresses and skirts that her mother bought for her were much too small. Anna went to her room and had a pity party. Her mother did not even know what size clothing she wore.

When her mother called to wish Anna a merry Christmas, she was told of the mistake. She said that as soon as she could get away, she would exchange the gifts for the correct size. Anna wondered how long she had to wait to receive her Christmas gifts.

Grammom and Papa Joe gave all of the girls new underwear for Christmas. The other girls wore their new clothing to church that Sunday. Anna wore her old clothing over the new underwear that she received as a Christmas gift.

Chapter 13

Family history passed down from one generation to the other was as follows: Papa Joe was Aunt Janie's brother. Their parents were freed slaves who traveled to Philadelphia during the Great Migration after the slaves were freed by proclamation. Papa Joe and Aunt Janie's parents had been slaves who lived on a plantation in the South. They acquired their family name from the plantation owner.

Papa Joe brought his parents to Philadelphia to live with him in West Philadelphia. The great-grandfather refused to wear shoes. He would walk to Market Street in his bare feet, return, sit on the porch, and prop his dirty feet on the railing.

When neighbors complained, he told them he was a free man and could do what he wanted. He lived to be eighty-nine years old. His wife was a quiet, complacent person who loved sitting in her rocking chair and singing softly. She died at age eighty-four.

Papa Joe, in his words, was a "godly man," even though he did not attend any church on a regular basis. He did not drink alcoholic beverages (maybe a little wine for the stomach's sake). He was not a cursing man (as long as gosh-dabbit, dad-blamed, or doggone did not count). He did not approve of dancing for It was a sin. He did have a habit of smoking cigarettes.

On Sunday mornings at breakfast time, he gathered the family around the table and prayed the prayer that never ends. He would thank God for the sun, the moon, the stars, and the rain. He prayed for the beggar on the street, for the saved and the unsaved, and for all of the people in hospitals and prisons. He could go on and on while the biscuits were getting cold.

One Sunday morning, he really became carried away with his prayer that never ends. The girls were hungry. Grammom had to clear the table and get the girls off to Sunday school. Then she had to go to church. He continued with his long list of people for the Lord to bless. Grammom interrupted with a quiet "… and Lord, please bless my dear husband and let him finish this prayer before the food gets cold. Amen."

Anyone living with Papa Joe knew his rules. Sunday was a day of rest. No working, no ironing, or no sewing was allowed. Children could not jump rope on the Lord's day. The girls played Old Maid card game during the week, but not on Sundays. "In six days, God made heaven and Earth, and on the seventh day, he rested" was his biblical quotation. Sunday was his religious seventh day.

He played gospel music on the radio on Sundays. This was typical in black neighborhoods in the early 1940s. One could walk down the street in most northern cities and hear gospel music blaring from radios in many homes.

Anna recalled the time when Grammom allowed the older girls to invite friends over early one Saturday afternoon. They were to arrive at 1:30 in the afternoon and leave around 5:00, before the man of the house came home at 6:00. She made punch and cookies. One of the boys brought a portable record player and records with him. They removed a large area rug from the living room floor and they danced the jitterbug, which was popular at that time. The girls were so happy because they would be popular at school since they were allowed to have a party.

About 4:00, the front door opened and in walked Papa Joe. He came home early that day. The music was playing and the boys and girls were dancing. He paused and gasped as if shocked. Then he announced, "The devil is in my house and I want to get him out of my house right now.

Shut that dadblame music thing off!" One of the boys went for the door, Papa Joe blocked him. "You young "uns put my rug back on the floor where it belongs and leave my house. I am a godly man and I will not have the devil's work in my home." He proceeded to the kitchen and closed the door. Just imagine the tongue lashing he was giving his wife behind that kitchen door. There were no more parties after that.

The girls were embarrassed when they returned to school. A few of the children were told of the incident. Several of the boys passed Anna in the school hallway and asked, "How is the godly man today?"

Before long, that episode was forgotten and more exciting days were to follow.

CHAPTER 14

Papa Joe was an enthusiast of Joe Louis, who was referred to as the Brown Bomber. He became excited whenever Joe Louis had a fight. There were no televisions in those days. The family would gather together in front of the only radio in the house.

Joe Louis was the heavyweight champion of the world from 1937 until 1949. He defeated all twenty of his challengers, including the German, Max Schmelling, whom he defeated three times. Schmelling was viewed as a Nazi symbol. Those were times preceding the Second World War.

When Joe Louis won his fights, Anna remembered, people in her neighborhood would go outside and bang on pots and pans. Some had noisemakers celebrating Joe

Louis's victories. It was like New Year's Eve. Papa Joe really enjoyed the fights.

The morning of Sunday, December 7, 1941, Anna's family enjoyed their usual Sunday morning breakfast without any incident. That morning, the radio was not on. The girls went to Sunday school. Grammom joined them in the main sanctuary for the Sunday morning service.

Before the minister delivered the sermon, he said he had very important news to announce to the congregation. "How many people listened to your radios this morning?" he asked. A few hands went up. "Then some of you are aware of what I am about to say. "My heart is saddened by the news this morning. Japanese planes fired upon our battleships at Pearl Harbor. Five of eight ships were destroyed and at least 2,400 Americans were killed. This will affect everyone in this room. This action will cause our great nation to enter into a war in which many will be killed. Let us pray." He prayed a long and powerful prayer for the souls of the deceased and their families, that they somehow would be comforted in their loss. He prayed for the United States of America and all who will be saddened in some way by that strike on Pearl Harbor. People cried openly that morning.

The announcement was repeated the next day, on Monday December 8, 1941, at Anna's school. Anna remembered it clearly as though it had just happened.

There were assemblies at her school so that everyone could hear President Roosevelt's speech to the nation.

He began with "Yesterday, December 7, 1941, a day that will live in infamy, the United States was suddenly attacked--." Those words were etched in Anna's mind for a very long time. Many young people who were seated in that high school auditorium later went to war. Some were killed and many more were injured physically or mentally. December 7, 1941 was a sad day for America.

CHAPTER 15

Anna overheard some of the older people's whispered conversations, which included unfavorable character assassinations against her mother. Once when her mother's name was mentioned, she walked into the kitchen where they were talking. The conversation ceased as she entered the room. That gave her an uneasy feeling. She was fifteen years of age and extremely sensitive. She had a feeling that she did not belong there.

Anna skipped two grades during her early years of schooling, and continued to do well scholastically. She was the youngest of her peers in high school and was proud of the fact that she would graduate high school at the age of sixteen.

The school years were divided in to two sessions, A and B. She was completing 12A and only had to complete 12B to graduate when she returned to school in September after the summer vacation. She was scheduled to graduate in February of the following year.

Every Saturday, her step-grandmother and one of the girls would strip the beds and spray the mattresses and springs to kill bedbugs. They had to spray around the baseboards of the walls and anywhere they felt the insects would lay eggs. Bedbugs are tiny, wingless, reddish-brown insects. They infested many homes during the 1940s. They existed all over town and did not discriminate. They were everywhere.

As she worked with Grammom, Anna casually asked why the elders were saying such horrible things about her mother. The grandmother asked what made her think they were saying such things about Sue. Anna spoke of the times when all conversation stopped when she entered a room after overhearing some of their conversation.

"I have no idea what you are talking about, young lady. And if you weren't so sneaky trying to hear adult conversation, you would not be making up stories like that." Anna retorted, slowly raising her voice, "You are well aware of what I am talking about. Now who is being sneaky pretending not to know?"

That last remark from Anna really riled the older lady. She started with, "You have your nerve, speaking to me that way. You are fifteen years old, and it is about time you realized a few things about your mother. First of all, she left you here, paying us nothing for your support. Does she care if you have food to eat or lunch money for school?

"Everyone knows why your father left your mother. He was a good man and tried to love her until he found out more about her lifestyle. We all know why she left Manuel. He was too good for her. He does not like wild parties and getting drunk. She likes to be around people who use filthy language and throw wild, drunken parties. Manuel is too domesticated for her.

"I watch you around boys your age. You are going to be no good, just like your mother. A leaf does not fall too far from the tree."

Anna stood there, awestruck. This lady is saying all of these nasty things to a daughter about her mother. She should not be talking to a daughter this way even if the mother did those bad things," she thought. Anna replied, "You hate my mother and you hate me. You are a mean old lady to say things like that to me. I hate you."

"You don't talk to me that way, young lady," her step-grandmother shouted. She rushed over to Anna and began slapping the teenager's face repeatedly. Anna raised her hands to ward off the blows, and a scuffle ensued.

Anna pulled away and ran to her room, screaming that she did not want to stay there anymore. Her face was stinging and extremely painful. She called a friend of her mother's and said that if her mother did not come and get her, she would run away because she was not welcome in that house.

The next day, Sue went to West Philadelphia and reluctantly took her daughter back to South Philly with her. She did what she had to do, because where would a fifteen-year-old girl go if she ran away from home? Sue had no alternative. They rented a room from a friend who lived on Carpenter Street near Twenty-first. They were very comfortable there.

Anna was not pleased with the fact that her school records had been transferred to a South Philadelphia high school that was a long distance from where she lived. She had to walk through areas that she did feel were safe for her. Her mother refused to pay public transportation fare for her to attend the new school, saying that Anna could walk that distance. Anna refused to go. She wished that she had stayed in West Philadelphia.

Anna's mother had given birth to another daughter when Anna was eighteen months old. Sue was just twenty-one when the second child was born. A short time later, she and her young husband separated. Her Aunt Janie took Anna with her and a neighbor offered to care for the other child on a weekly basis. There were times when Sue failed to pick up her youngest on weekends as was pre-arranged.

The neighbor loved the little girl and decided that she would move out of state with the child and leave no forwarding address. She felt that Sue was an inappropriate mother. She changed the child's name to Grace and they lived as mother and daughter.

After Sue and her husband reconciled, many of their arguments concerned the whereabouts of his other daughter. Sue never reported the child missing or tried to find her youngest child. That was a mystery to Anna for years.

Sue occasionally attended a Baptist church on Carpenter Street. One Sunday. she noticed a lady with a girl of about Anna's age attending a church service. The lady's face looked familiar. Two weeks later, the same two were at church again. Sue asked Anna to sit next to them and ask the girl her name and age. Armed with that information, Sue approached the lady and called her by name. Realizing who Sue was, the lady almost fainted. Sue calmed her down and said she wanted to cause no trouble. "Just let my daughter know who I am and allow her to her to know her sister. My goodness, they look almost like twins."

There were overnight visits. The foster mother was cordial but not at all pleased with the situation. Soon they moved away to a small town in New Jersey. Anna and her sister corresponded by mail occasionally, but never visited one anther again. They remained in New Jersey until Anna's sister graduated high school and enrolled in a North Jersey college. She dated a South African student. After their graduation, they married and went to Africa to live. The two sisters corresponded for a short time. A few years later, Grace's husband notified Anna in a letter that her sister had died of cancer.

Chapter 16

After a few months, Sue decided to move again. She kept late hours and did not want to continue disturbing the household, returning home after everyone else was in bed. When Sue put her key in the door, the landlord would call out loudly, "Sue, is that you?" Other tenants would tease her about keeping such late hours.

She found another apartment on Sixteenth Street near Catherine Street. This one was on the second floor with a private bath. They were returning to large three-story houses converted into apartments exclusively for poor people. Anna was experiencing a feeling of deja vu

Her mother bought an old iron bed and a dresser for the bedroom, two chairs, and a kitchen table from a used furniture store on South Street. A wooden icebox left behind by a previous tenant. It had a pan beneath it to catch water from the melting ice. A friend gave her a folding cot and a straight-back chair that she placed in the front room (the living room).

The floors were bare. Laundry had to be washed in the bathtub by hand, using a metal washboard and hung out to dry. Any day, one could see many pulley lines with varied articles of clothing swaying in the wind behind those big three-story buildings.

Anna's mother had one set of sheets for her bed, which Anna washed by hand in the bathtub using the washboard and brown Octagon soap, that people often used for laundry in those days. She would hang the laundry out the window on a pulley line that extended to a pole in the back of the yard. Breakfast was usually cornflakes and milk. A Chinese restaurant was on the corner where Anna was sent at times to buy a fish sandwich and a bottle of soda for supper. They often had canned pork and beans and hot dogs boiled in water for their evening meal.

There was an organization on South Broad Street where poor people would get a nice meal for twenty-five cents. They had a large projection room upstairs where diners could watch movies of properties owned by the leader of that group. Anna thought the group also owned a hotel on North Broad Street where they rented rooms at reasonable rates. There was no cohabitation. Men and women had separate quarters.

These are Anna's childhood memories. They may or may not be accurate. They are her memories. These things are things she remembers. After all, she was almost ninety years of age at the time of the interview. However, her memory seemed crystal clear on a number of things.

Chapter 17

For those unfamiliar with the layout of streets in the city of Philadelphia, what normally would have been named Fourteenth Street is named Broad Street, and it is situated between Thirteenth and Fifteenth streets. It is an exceptionally wide thoroughfare and is one of the main parade routes.

Two major department stores that were very popular in the 1930s and 1940s are no longer there. They are Gimbel Brothers at Eighth and Market streets and John Wannamaker's, on Market Street East opposite City Hall.

Anna used to walk a few blocks to Broad Street to watch the parades. The Thanksgiving Day parade was the shortest. It included many floats and marching bands, including some local high school bands. There were a number of string bands in the Thanksgiving Day parade. That parade preceded the Christmas season and probably continued to do so for many years.

Santa Claus's elves and old Santa himself appeared at the end of the parade. He waved at the children as the elves pranced along collecting Christmas lists from little children along the parade route. In Anna's day, the parade ended at Gimbel's department store, where good old Santa would climb a fire truck ladder into the building where children would visit him until Christmas Eve.

The biggest parade was and probably still is the New Year's Day parade. Spectators had to arrive very early to secure a spot to stand and watch it. Some would bring wooden crates to sit on. Blankets, mufflers, and earmuffs were essential for the cold winter weather. There were bleachers erected in Center City for people to sit and watch the parades. New Year's Day parades lasted all day. There were comic sections and string bands that competed for prizes. Anna recalls seemingly endless numbers of string bands adorned with regal costumes and feathers of every color imaginable. The comic section consisted of whiteface and blackface mimes marching along, doing the mummer's strut. She thought that the festivities continued into the night hours.

There were smaller parades within the African-American community in which a number of local bands participated. Sue remembered that her mother was a member of one of the marching bands. She proudly smiled and winked at her daughter and friends as her unit marched along the parade route on Christian Street. Many watched from apartment windows, while others lined the sidewalk cheering.

Chapter 18

Neighborhood kids in underprivileged neighborhoods in those days had very little planned activity. There seemed to be no Little League or Boy Scout troops in the area where Anna resided. If there were, parents did not know about them. Many children did not have families who took the time to be with their children. So many parents simply fed their kids and gave them a place to sleep. That is why so many kids got into trouble devising their own means of entertainment.

Trolleys provided a source of amusement for some of the kids. Power was generated to the cars by means of a pole atop each trolley. When one would stop at a corner to take on or discharge passengers, one of the children would pull the pole from the overhead wire, cutting off the power, including inside lights. The motorman or conductor had to go around to the back of the trolley to replace the pole on the overhead wire. This annoyed motormen and passengers as well.

In the summer, they had another prank. Windows of all trolleys were open to get air during hot weather. They had no air conditioners. Someone would open a fireplug on the corner for children to play in the water and cool off. If one positioned his buttocks at a certain angle, the water would forcefully flow into the open windows of a trolley, soaking unsuspecting passengers.

Some of the children hopped rides on the sides of trolleys by getting a grip on an open window. That could be extremely dangerous. It was said that a girl lost both legs doing that. She fell and her legs were caught beneath the wheels of the car and were severed.

There were train tracks on Washington Avenue nearby where manufactured goods were shipped to other parts of the country. Trains moved slowly along that street. Kids often played around trains and hopped rides on them with no regard for loss of life or limb.

There were at least five families living in each apartment building. Their mailboxes and doorbells were in unlocked entranceways. Some smart kid would stick a pin in every doorbell in a building, causing it to ring until the occupants came out of their units to remove the pin. It was fun for the door ringer, who stood at a distance, laughing at angry residents who came to the door, annoyed, angry, and often cursing.

Yes, kids in that day in poor neighborhoods had many pranks. Some were even acts of vandalism.

CHAPTER 19

Once, South Street near Broad Street was predominantly an African-American neighborhood. Businesses included Jewish stores, Chinese restaurants, a few black-owned businesses, and secondhand stores selling used furniture to the poor.

The old South Street was a favorite place for night life (mostly neighborhood residents). There were bars and nightclubs in the area. There was a VFW post on that street. Around the corner from South Street was the Lincoln Theatre, where Anna and her young friends saw a number of big bands of the Jazz Era. They also saw a number of live performers at the Earle Theatre in Center City.

Anna remembered seeing Cab Calloway in his white suit, singing "Minnie the Moocher" and other favorites of the time. Duke Ellington and his band played there as well. She remembered the comic Dusty Fletcher singing "Open the Door, Richard," which became a popular song very often played on local radio stations.

A children's talent show was broadcast from the Lincoln Theatre every Sunday morning. Many talented young singers performed on that show. A teenager with a melodious voice opened the show, singing the old Negro spiritual, "Deep River, My Home Is Over Jordan."

There was a record store on South Street near Fifteenth, where Anna recalled seeing a very young Ella Fitzgerald promoting her recording "A Tisket, a Tasket, I Lost my Yellow Basket." She sang with Chick Webb's orchestra. Later, he died at an early age. Many famous musicians performed on the stage at the Earle Theatre in Center City. Attending a performance there usually called for wearing their finest. For people from Anna's area in South Philly, it was a big deal to travel to Center City Theatre and enjoy live performances by famous entertainers of the Jazz Era.

Although Anna was aware of the nightlife in her day, she was too young at the time to become involved in it. She enjoyed music of the times and felt that was an era to be remembered. In her old age, at the time of her interview with Jake Spencer, she occasionally hummed a tune or two from the 1940s.

CHAPTER 20

The inactive teenager began to get bored with her surroundings. She was locked into a situation over which she had very little control. She and her mother no longer attended a church. It was just the two of them. They should have been companions and done some things together. That never happened.

Often she lay awake night, listening for the sound of her mother's key opening the door. Sue sometimes returned home under the influence of alcohol and would immediately pass out on the cot in the front room. At least, she was at home and those were times when Anna was not at home alone.

Often, when Anna would sit in that bare apartment, she wished that her mother did not keep such late hours.

When Sue first brought Anna to that section of town, Anna was a six-year-old little girl and unaccustomed to poverty. Then she was temporarily removed to a place where life was much better for her. Again as a teenager, she was brought back into the same unfortunate situation.

She observed the destitution among her neighbors and had empathy for them until reality set in. She realized the fact that she was just as poor as they. The difference was that she had once lived better than they. Now she longed to return to that better life she once knew.

A series of questions saturated her mind. What if Aunt Janie had not gone to be with the Lord? What if Grammom had not said those horrible things about her mother? (Even if there may have been some truth in what she said.) Why was she rude to Grammom? What if she had stayed with her grandfather and completed her high school education? She should be in college then. She had many crying spells.

Her mother bought cake and ice cream for her sixteenth birthday and sang "Happy Birthday" to her. She received a very pretty blouse (the correct size) as a gift.

Anna took a couple cleaning jobs in homes in the northeast section of the city. Her very first job was cleaning houses in the Roosevelt Boulevard section of the city. Then she saw an ad in the local newspaper, advertising for a messenger with the old Postal Telegraph Company. She delivered telegrams to offices in Center City. Her hours were 9:00 AM until 5:00 PM and was paid forty-five cents per hour.

She gave her mother most of the money from her paycheck and kept just enough for carfare, lunch money, and a few personal items. Her mother also found a better job, pressing clothes in a laundry during the day. Many evenings she would come home, bathe, get dressed, go out, and return extremely late. Sometimes a male friend would accompany her home.

Neighbors were aware of the fact that Sue returned home very late at night, leaving her young daughter alone. A specific nineteen-year-old neighbor and others sat on the front steps with Anna early evenings, socializing. One night, that young man lingered longer than the others.

They sat and talked. He was attractive and she liked him. Soon he began buying her ice-cream cones. She thought that he was a really nice guy. He even kissed her good night. "Oh, he was a smooth operator," remarked Anna to the journalist.

Then he began his strategy. He asked to accompany her to her apartment since they had become friends. Soon he began ringing her doorbell evenings when Anna did not go out to sit on the front steps. His affectionate demeanor allured Anna.

She felt as though at least someone loved her. Yes, he loved her so much that one day Sue noticed that her daughter was pregnant. There was no justification for Anna's yielding to temptation. She knew what she was doing was the wrong thing to do. She made a bad decision and would pay very dearly for her indiscretion for years to come. Anna said that when we make mistakes, we are not to blame others.

Anna told her mother about her night visitor. When Sue approached the neighbor's mother concerning her son's impending fatherhood, the mother responded that any one of those men bringing Sue home nights could have fathered her daughter's baby, and asked, "Why blame my son?"

She failed to mention that her son was the accused father of another neighborhood girl's yet unborn child. It seems that he may have been ringing more than one doorbell. The other young lady moved in with that family and remained there until after the son was drafted into the army during World War II.

CHAPTER 21

Sue and her daughter sat down and had a serious conversation. The mother stated, "In a few months, you will be showing and unable to keep your Postal Telegraph job. I do not earn enough money to support three people. Now just what do you expect to do about it?"

That was the first serious down-to-earth mother-and-daughter conversation they had ever had. They should have been seriously talking many months before that situation occurred. Where was she when Anna needed adult supervision? The girl needed a mother, not a roommate. Anna told her mother that she would find another job.

Anna asked for a day off from her job and went searching for another. Success came on the very first day. She was hired as packer of children's clothing at a manufacturing company in a building at Broad and Carpenter streets. Then she and her mother moved to another apartment on Webster Street near Twenty-first Street. She was able to walk that distance to work. She was a good employee began to draw regular checks. She now earned fifty cents an hour.

Again she gave her mother all she earned except for bare essentials for her personal needs. That compensated for the time when she would be unable to work until her baby was a few months old. At work, she wore oversized, loose fitting clothing. Only those with whom she worked closely were aware of her condition.

A part-time male employee who was born in Virginia began to take a special interest in Anna. He asked to escort her to a movie in Center City, and she gave him a negative reply. She assumed he had an ulterior motive. When he approached her again, she told him that she was not dating because of her impending motherhood. Surprised, he questioned her concerning the father of the child. She explained the situation and he seemed quite sympathetic.

Later, he invited her to attend his church with him on the following Sunday. She did, and to her surprise, that Sunday he preached his trial sermon to become a Baptist minister. He spoke eloquently. Anna was extremely impressed and actually admired him.

A few days later, he explained that he was attracted to her because of her personality. He told Anna that a nice lady like her had many unpleasant circumstances ahead of her as an unwed mother. He was willing to marry her, to help raise her child in a good Christian environment, if she would give him a chance to really know him.

She dwelled on the words, "really get to know him" and wondered what that aspiring preacher had in mind. She tried to visualize how her life might have been had she not allowed herself to have a stigma placed upon herself because of her pregnancy. She realized that she had fallen, and it was imperative that she rise and face her responsibilities. The young man was too upright to bear the shame of her indiscretions.

Anna gave it plenty of thought and decided not to accept his offer. She prudently explained her reason to him. The subject never came up again. Apparently, he also had given it plenty of thought for a short time lately. He terminated his employment there and went away.

Anna was a good worker. She never took time off from work. Her employers were very fond of her and treated her well. She was in her sixth month of pregnancy when they noticed her condition. She continued working until she went into labor and was transported to a city-owned general hospital.

At the tender age of seventeen, she gave birth to a healthy six-pound-two-ounce baby girl. A nurse placed the cute little bundle wrapped in a pink receiving blanket into Anna's arms, and the young mother was thrilled with that beautiful child. She cuddled her newborn and whispered, "You are so sweet. You do not deserve a life as complicated as your mother's has been. I hope yours will be much better." Then, displaying a faint smile, she repeated the word hope. "Yes, Hope, that is the name that I will give you. You are my little Hope."

CHAPTER 22

In the meantime, the Philadelphia Transportation Company (PTC) was experiencing a serious labor problem. For years since its inception, driver positions were reserved only for white employees. Men of color were hired exclusively in menial positions. The situation exploded when the company hired its very first Negro driver. On August 4, 1944, almost ten thousand white PTC drivers walked off their jobs in protest.

The strike lasted only one week. The public walked, carpooled, hitchhiked, and resorted to any means available to reach their places of employment. Approximately 3 million man-hours of labor were lost during that time. Many workers were employed in the war effort, for the country was in World War II at the time.

Many of the people affected by the strike worked for the Philadelphia Navy Yard, Frankford Arsenal, Bendix Aviation, Army Quarter Quartermasters, and other related employers.

President Franklin D. Roosevelt sent troops to Philadelphia to drive the buses and trolleys. The strike had an adverse effect on the war effort. After the strike was settled, troops remained aboard the public vehicles until calm was restored, for there was much tension between the races because of the strike. Anna could remember all of that, for it happened in her lifetime when Hope was a newborn.

She also remembered an embarrassing situation that happened to her during World War II. Ladies' underpants were held up by means of buttons instead of elastic in their waistbands, because rubber was used in the war effort. While standing aboard a transit bus one day, a button holding her underwear suddenly popped off, causing her panties to slowly dislodge from her waist. They slid down both legs and ended around her ankles. With people all around her, she quickly bent over and slipped first one foot and then another out of her panties and placed them in her handbag. She looked at no one, and exited at the very next stop.

On a lighter side, before the war, American ladies wore silk stockings. Because silk was used to make parachutes, etc., it was no longer available for the manufacture of ladies' silk stockings. For probably the first time, it became fashionable for women to go barelegged. They began applying leg makeup of varied hues to their legs. Silk stockings at that time had seams down the backs of their legs. To give the appearance of seams, ladies would draw a straight line with an eyebrow pencil down the backs of their legs. It seemed a bit ridiculous, but the aged Anna recalled how she also used to do that.

CHAPTER 23

Owners of the factory had agreed to allow Anna to return to work whenever she was able. Little Hope was eight weeks old when Anna began working again. She became a wage earner again, a fact that pleased her mother. The young mother had a daughter to support.

She was told of a young married mother who lived one block from the factory where she worked, who was willing to care for the newborn on a daily basis. Anna's mother had purchased a used crib and baby carriage for the baby.

Each morning, rain or shine, Anna got up, fed her baby, and packed necessary items, and then went off to the babysitter's and then to work. It was a six-city-block walk to the babysitter's apartment, which was on the third floor of her building.

The baby buggy had to be folded and taken up two flights of stairs and brought down again in the evenings. The procedure was repeated where Anna lived, for she also lived in a third-floor apartment. She had to wash little Hope's cloth diapers by hand and hang them out to dry.

One day, some of Anna's co-workers asked Anna to go on boat ride with them on the Wilson Line, which was a showboat that traveled along the Delaware River. When Anna asked her mother to care for Hope while she was away, Sue answered, "It's your baby; take care of her yourself. I don't have any babies."

The babysitter agreed to care for Hope. Anna went with her friends and had a relaxing day away from work and the care of her baby. She and her babysitter began to help one another occasionally. This gave each of them a little time off to relax.

Anna felt that it was time for her to move on. She questioned her mother's love for her and the child. She felt unloved. She and her mother hardly ever talked unless it was about money. Sue was out most of the time. Anna realized that she could support herself and her baby. She decided it was time to move on. She began searching for another place to live.

Chapter 24

There was a lady who lived near Fifteenth on Naudain Street, who rented a room to another young unwed mother. Naudain Street is a small street just north of South Street. Anna was told that she could stay there and did not have to take her small child out in all kinds of weather. She inquired, and the kind lady took Anna and Hope into her modest home.

To Anna's surprise, the house had running water in the kitchen but no bathroom facility. The toilet was in a shed in the back yard. At night, they had to use covered containers in their bedrooms to relieve themselves. The next morning, those pots were emptied into the toilet in the back yard, passing through the kitchen.

The three-story house had two rooms on each floor. The landlady slept in the front room on the first floor, and the kitchen was in the back. There were two bedrooms each on the second and third floors. Passing through one was required to get to the other. This type of house was referred to in those days as an "ace deuce and trey."

Bedrooms had pitchers and basins for sponging between tub baths, which were taken in tin tubs in the kitchen. That room was closed off whenever one took a bath. Water was heated on a coal-burning stove in the kitchen, which was also used for cooking. Many similar houses were in areas where poor people lived in those days.

Neighbors were carefree. Many lived in squalor without realizing there could be a better way of life. Children still played the usual childhood games of that time, such as jump rope and jacks. Disgruntled youngsters sometimes engaged in fisticuffs, having observed their elders settle disputes in like manner. Old men gathered at card tables, playing cards or checkers, drinking beer, and laughing uproariously.

Once when Anna was returning home, she heard the sound of scuffling feet behind her on the opposite side of Naudain Street. Then she heard gunshots. There were no porches attached to houses. The only place of refuge for her was to run up the three steps of a house and stand in the doorway. She had Hope with her. She placed her baby in front of her and turned her back to the street. There she stood in fear for her baby's life and her own.

A man ran past and fell on the ground. Another caught up to him and fired two or three more shots into the one on the ground and ran off toward Sixteenth Street and disappeared. After a few seconds, the one on the ground slowly got up and stumbled in the direction of Fifteenth Street, leaving a trail of blood drops.

A shaken Anna was terrified by what she had witnessed. When she regained her composure, she continued to return home with the baby in her arms.

It distressed her very much to see how those people existed. Her home in West Philadelphia was never like where she was then living. She wished that she could return to her grandfather's house. She had a chance to experience people's fate in all walks of life. Some get trapped in their surroundings and remain there. Others with the same background set goals for themselves and move on to a better life. They had to realize that there was a better life away from their underprivileged environment.

Anna had empathy for those around her, for she personally was walking in their shoes. She met many good people trapped in those unfortunate circumstances. Having experienced their plight, she was gaining an education in human relations that no text-book could ever divulge. She could definitely say that she understood how it feels to live under unfavorable circumstances.

There are varied reasons for people's difficulties in life. Those better off financially could be more benevolent in their sharing. Many churches and charitable organizations do assist the poor; also disadvantaged ones have to have the desire to be helped.

A quote from King James Version of the Holy Bible, Luke 14;13 reads, "But when thou makest a feast, call the poor, the maimed, the lame, the blind. Luke 14:14, "And thou shall be blessed; for they cannot recompence thee: for thou shall be recompenced at the resurrection of the just". In other words, reach out and help those who cannot help themselves, without expecting any reward.

That area of Naudain Street and the surrounding areas were later redeveloped and included in the Society Hill section of Philadelphia. The renovated homes were priced so high that poor people who once lived there could no longer return to a place they once called home, giving the appearance of poor people being replaced by the affluent. Could this be a form of gentrification?" Anna queried silently.

CHAPTER 25

One day, a middle-aged lady at work became concerned about Anna's situation and decided to have a motherly talk with the young pregnant lady during a lunch break. She said that Anna seemed above average in intelligence. She should continue her education and take her rightful place in society if she so desired.

The environment that Anna had chosen was not adequate for her and her little daughter, who deserved a better way of life. "What can I do?" Anna asked. "I have no moral support from anyone, including my own mother. I refuse to go on welfare as so many young mothers around here are doing. I would rather work and earn a living for my child. I cannot continue my education. I have a child to support."

As the conversation proceeded, the co-worker told Anna about friends of hers who wanted to have children. The wife experienced two miscarriages and was told that she was unable to bear children. Anna interrupted, "Stop right there, lady. I am not giving up my daughter to strangers. End of conversation." Anna then walked away.

Months passed, and Anna could not forget her talk with that kind lady on her job. She began to think about her situation. Her landlady, when asked, agreed to care for her baby when Anna enrolled in Standard Evening High School on North Broad Street.

She attended and later graduated with an academic diploma. After graduation, the counselor asked if she could help Anna get into a college. She offered to help the young graduate obtain financial aid. Anna said that was impossible at that time.

She invited her mother to her high school graduation ceremony. "Now you can get a better-paying job," her mother told her. Those were not the words she needed to hear from her mother. Somehow, she expected praise for her accomplishment. All that was on that lady's mind was money.

Soon the interested co-worker approached Anna again. This time she invited Anna to attend her church with her the following Sunday. Anna had not attended any church for a long time and readily accepted.

It was a very large church on South Broad Street, not far from Washington Avenue. It had an exceptionally large seating capacity, including a balcony. The pipe organ, with its glistening pipes, extended high up on the walls. Its encompassing melodious sounds emanated throughout the huge sanctuary, reminding Anna of that magnificent pipe organ she used to hear in the center court of John Wanamaker's department Store.

A well-dressed, beautiful lady approached them after the service. She asked the co-worker for a ride home. The two seemed to know one another. She was introduced to Anna, who was asked if she minded if they drove the lady home before taking Anna back to Naudain Street. Anna agreed.

They arrived at the lady's home. When invited in, Anna readily accepted because she wanted to see the inside of the house. The home was lavishly furnished for a home in that vicinity. "These people must really be rich," Anna thought.

They were given a tour of the home. Anna expressed how lovely the house was. The lady said, "Lovely, yes; all it needs is the patter of little feet." The conversation proceeded to the fact that she and her husband were the couple Anna was told about who wanted to adopt a baby.

Now Anna had been thinking about how nice it would be if she could go to college. What future could she give Hope in her present situation? Then again, how could she work, attend college, study and care for Hope at the same time?

She had been thinking about possibly giving her child up for adoption but not to strangers. She asked the co-worker's friend, "If you adopted a baby, would you let her know her mother one day?" After a brief hesitation, the lady answered, "I would consider that."

Then Anna began to speak "My Hope would hate me if she thought that I did not love her and gave her away. Then again, where we are now, either of us could be killed or raped or something. Maybe I should let someone adopt her and give her a chance to have a good life." She became teary-eyed.

The nice lady embraced Anna and said, "My dear, no one is pressuring you to give up your baby. We are on the adoption list, and soon we will have a precious little baby to love and care for. You appear to be a loving mother. Any decision you make concerning your daughter will have to be made by you alone. Go home. Get on your knees and pray. Ask God to lead you in the right direction.

We cannot always make wise decisions on our own. There are times when we need divine intervention, for He said, 'Lo, I am with you always.(Matt 28:20) My dear, let go of your anguish and let God lead you. He is able to lead you in the right direction."

For many days after that meeting, the young mother got on her knees and prayed constantly. "God, I place my problem in your hands. Lead me and guide me in this difficult situation." Relieved that she was asking the right one for help, she stopped worrying and went about her daily activities, still praying. She had taken her worries out of her hands and placed them into the hands of God.

Early one morning, a small voice within her said, "Allow Hope to live a better life. You cannot give her the life that she deserves. If you really love her, let her go." She felt that must have been the voice of Jesus. She began thanking God, for she truly felt He was answering her prayers, and this must have been the divine intervention she so needed.

Soon thereafter, she asked if the couple had adopted a baby yet and was told no; they were still praying that they would get one soon. Then she asked if she and Hope could visit the couple. At the very first meeting, Hope and the nice lady seemed to be a match made in heaven. The child cooed and lay in her potential adopted mother's arms. There were more visits. The husband was very affectionate with the child. Both husband and wife appeared to be falling in love with little Hope.

Each subsequent visit seemed to be better than the last. On one occasion, Sue told her landlady that her mother wanted to keep her baby over the weekend. She took her child to the couple that wanted to adopt her. When Anna returned to take her baby home, Hope cried as the wife was handing the baby over to Anna. It was obvious that the child would be in good hands.

Anna finally decided that giving the baby up was best for the child. It was out of her great love for her daughter that she handed the child over to the couple that would give her love and affection and a great environment in which to grow. They went through the adoption procedure and Hope had a new home.

Both birth mother and adoptive mother agreed to exchange Christmas cards each year, and at an appropriate time, by mutual agreement, Hope would meet her birth mother.

Chapter 26

Many poor families in those days never dreamed of giving up their children for adoption. Even if they had ten or twelve, they managed to keep them. Children of very large poor families had a hard life growing up and they survived. Many did very well in adult life.

She had only one child and gave her away. She realized that it was out of love that she made the right choice. She often wished her own mother had given her up for adoption. Her life may have much better. She realized that her sister was with someone who gave her a lot of love and nurturing. She was almost jealous of her own sister for that reason. Anna moved again, renting a room near her job because of harsh criticism she was receiving from her landlady about giving her child up.

She later visited the school counselor, who arranged for her to enter a college of her choice. She had passed all of the entrance exams with high scores. Then, asked if she wanted to attend a local university on North Broad Street, she declined. She preferred to go as far away from Philadelphia as she could get.

Anna was enrolled in a Southern all-black university, tuition free. She was required to work on the campus, and she was happy to do that. At midterm and Christmas holidays, she visited the homes of other students. She had no home of her own to visit. She studied very hard and completed four years of academic studies in three years by enrolling in summer courses.

She and a male student, named Benjamin, became romantically involved. She told him of her daughter and circumstances concerning her adoption decision. He agreed that was the right thing to do. Otherwise he never would have met her. At graduation, he was her only supporter.

She felt that she had no family to cheer her on. Benjamin graduated ahead of her and rented an apartment off campus. World War II did not interrupt his studies, because it was discovered that he had a heart murmur. He was granted a deferment from the armed services. She moved into his apartment. Soon after that, they married and bought a home.

They were blessed with two boys, who were told of their sister in Philadelphia and that someday they would meet her. As the years passed, both Anna and Benjamin received their graduate degrees. Their children excelled scholastically as well.

Anna recalled the summer of 1963. She could never forget August 18, 1963, when she and her family boarded a chartered bus headed for Washington, D.C. Buses traveled from all parts of the country. They came by train, bus, automobile, or by any means possible to get to that great historical event, Martin Luther King Jr's March on Washington. It was to promote equal rights and to end discrimination against Negroes. Bias abounded throughout the country. There was discrimination in schools, restaurants, public restrooms, theaters, workplaces, churches, and even in burial grounds.

Little did she and her husband realize the significance of what they and their boys were about to witness. The enormity of it all was beyond comprehension. They exited their bus and very slowly moved along with the crowd toward the Lincoln Memorial, where they were told much of the activities would take place. She remembered just how friendly people were. Catholics, Protestants, the Nation of Islam, people of the Jewish faith, and many other denominations, black and white, all came together for unity.

The old lady Anna leaned forward toward the journalist and said, "Mr. Spencer, let me tell you about some of the celebrities who were there." She mentioned Marion Anderson, Ossie Davis, Sammy Davis Jr., Harry Belafonte, Lena Horn, Sidney Poitier, and of course, Rosa Parks, who had refused to give up her seat on a bus to a white person. She sparked a citywide bus boycott by Negroes in Montgomery, Alabama. There were so many well-known people that she could not possibly name all of them. She and her husband were just thrilled to see all of those important people.

As a retired school teacher, history was foremost in her mind, even in her advanced years. The family returned home, thanking God for allowing them to be a part of that momentous occasion and for returning home safely. She remembered that it was a most peaceful gathering of so many people of varied backgrounds.

Both Anna and her husband became born-again Christians. Her husband told her that nothing should separate her from the love of Christ. Separating herself from her family could alienate her from her Master's love. How could Martin Luther King Jr. bring harmony and togetherness to so many people when there was no harmony between family members?

He reminded her in the gospel of Matthew that when Peter asked how many times must he forgive his brother, the answer was not seventy but seventy-seven times seven. Then he asked her if she had forgiven her family for things that occurred in the past. She said that she had and that she intended to make amends. In the meantime, they became caught up in daily activities of teaching and raising their children, and she procrastinated.

Then in 1965, she was notified of PaPa Joe's death. She hastily prepared to return to Philadelphia. There she was reunited with her mother and Grammom, her step-grandmother. They hugged and kissed and were very pleased to see one another. Anna apologized to Grammom for her actions as a teenager, and was told that those were in the past and they didn't need to ever mention it again. "I said some things that were not very nice as well," her step-grandmother admitted.

Later, they sat together at the repast. It was extremely pleasant to note the Christian love and forgiveness among them. Years had erased any hard feelings that may have existed. The saying is, "To err is human, to forgive is divine."

One day in 1985, someone rang Anna's doorbell. When she answered, there stood a beautiful young lady who asked to see Miss Anna. She has been seeing Christmas cards from her mother's friend, Miss Anna, and remembered the return address. While visiting a school friend in the area, she thought she would surprise her mother by calling on her mother's old friend. Anna asked the young lady her name. To her surprise, the young lady's name was Hope Jamison. She was Anna's daughter, whom she had tearfully given away in adoption.

"Please come in," a surprised Anna said. "Are your parents Mr. and Mrs. Jamison of Philadelphia, Pennsylvania? Are you their only child?"

Hope answered, "Yes, they told me that I was adopted, but that doesn't matter, because we are a very happy family. I am so glad that they adopted me. Why do you ask?"

After a long pause, Anna said, "Hope, I am your birth mother." She walked over and embraced the surprised young lady. They held on to each other for quite a while before either of them could speak, for now they were both teary-eyed. Hope spoke first. "Mom told me that Miss Anna was her best friend because she did something very nice for her many years ago. One time, she told me that I would meet my birth mother one day. Oh my goodness, this is the day. I am so happy to finally meet you."

Anna called her sons and said, "Boys, here is your big sister that we told you about." The boys were elated. There was a great show of affection. Then Anna's husband came into the room. That was a wonderful time for all of them.

Hope told them that she was so very glad that she had stopped by. She could not stop smiling. "I want to call my mom. Oh my goodness, I have two moms now." She called her mother and told her the good news. They were all pleased that Hope had met her birth mother.

When Anna and her daughter had a chance to talk privately, Hope told her mother not to regret what she had done. She had been told that she was given up out of love and so that she could have a better life. Hope said, "I will always love you for what you have done for me. You are my mom, Anna."

Anna told her daughter that there were special people who lived in Philadelphia for her to meet. They were Anna's mother, Sue, and Grammom, her step-grandmother, (PaPa Joe's widow). "Those two are very old now and need our love and affection. We had unpleasant experiences when I was younger, but all is forgiven now and we love one another very much. Always remember John 15:12 in the Holy Bible: 'This is my commandment, that ye love one another as I have loved you.'"

Anna then asked, "How are things back in Philadelphia?" She referred to recent news at that time about homes being burned and eleven lives lost, including some children. A group of people objected to the way the system was treating minorities and formed a group voicing their opinions. They rented a house in West Philadelphia and lived together and protested publicly. Some of their members were arrested, and the group loudly voiced their concerns. Neighbors were annoyed over loud complaints voiced over bullhorns in their neighborhood.

On May 11, 1985, police went to that black middle-class neighborhood. Gunfire erupted and a bomb was dropped on their house, which had a bunker on the roof where gasoline may have been stored. It exploded and set off a fire that eventually burned an entire city block of homes on that street. (The episode is matter of public record.)

It was thought that an order to extinguish the fire was delayed. Anna remembered seeing the red glow in the sky that night, which could be seen for miles around.

They dwelled on that subject a little while until Hope remembered that she had friends waiting for her, and she reluctantly departed.

Anna then had three wonderful children. Hope had two loving mothers and two little brothers. Anna stated that she felt as though the heavens had opened up and God had smiled down upon her that day.

Anna retired as vice principal of her school after twenty-eight years of exemplary service. In his sixty-eighth year, her husband died of a massive heart attack. Their children married and moved out of state. They then had their own family responsibilities.

Old Anna was nearing ninety years of age, weak, and walking with a cane. She needed custodial care because she had fallen a number of times and was unable to get up unassisted. She opted to be placed in an assisted-living facility with only one stipulation: that she visit the homes of her children on weekends when it was convenient. At times, she stated that she needed to get away from those old people in the facility. She then chuckled at her own witticism, and they finally completed their series of interviews.

At a small reception given in her honor, Anna told of the many times she tried to tell her story, but those around her had little time to listen to the chatter of an old woman. When they first met, Mr. Spencer asked that she call him Jake. She responded, "Oh no, I could never do that. I don't know you that well." After the reception, Anna thanked Mr. Spencer for his patience with an old lady. She then smiled and slowly made her way down the hall, tapping her cane and repeating Martin Luther King Jr's words, "Free at last, free at last. Thank God Almighty, this old mind is free at last."

CHAPTER 27

One chilly morning, the journalist parked his car in a prison parking lot. He had obtained permission to interview an inmate for material he was compiling. He was working on a magazine article on the reason people turn to a life of crime. The warden had chosen a prisoner who seemed to be cooperating with officials and not causing any trouble among his peers. This man had been given twenty years for armed robbery. He was beginning year ten of his sentence.

The journalist wriggled from his car, locked the door, and proceeded slowly to the entrance. He could see armed guards at the top of a high wall that surrounded the prison. The men seemed to be watching his every move.

He tightened the scarf around his neck, as the wind was whipping at his face. My God, he thought, why am I doing this when I could be comfortably seated at my desk in a warm office? He pulled out a tissue and blew his nose, then rushed to the entrance to get out of the cold weather.

Inside there were families of inmates sitting on benches, waiting for their names to be called to visit loved ones. There were little children, possibly waiting to see their fathers. He pitied those little ones whose childhood memories consisted of going to prison to see their dads. He also saw lawyers with briefcases, there to help some unfortunate soul get out of that terrible place.

He signed in at the desk and was given the name of the person he was to interview. Then he waited to be called. Some visitors were talking loudly and had to be calmed down by the guard at the desk. A baby began crying, and the mother was attempting to console him. The journalist waited for about an hour before he was called to the desk. It seemed like an eternity.

Finally, the guard on duty at the front desk called him and he hastily responded. His credentials were checked, and a gate was electronically opened. He entered a small enclosure, where he was checked for weapons. His pockets and briefcase were searched. Then another electronic door was opened and he was escorted into the visitation room.

Two rows of seats were separated by a partition through which the interview would take place. The journalist faced an inmate who was already seated.

"Good morning; my name is Jake Spencer from the Weekly Express. I have been assigned to write a human-interest story about your life. I understand that you are aware of my mission and have agreed to talk with me. Is that correct?"

The answer was, "Yes, Mr. Spencer; my name is Alfred. You may call me Al; that is what my family and friends call me. I signed the release you left at the desk so that you may quote me on anything I say to you. To begin with, excuse my expression, but this place is hell."

Jake was unprepared to meet such an outspoken, amicable young man facing him. "What on earth caused this person to do something so drastic as to be confined in a place like this?" he asked himself. The inmate was small in stature and looked the journalist straight in the eye as they talked. He seemed calm and composed. His speech was flawless. Remembering that the inmate addressed him as Mr. Spencer, he said, "Al, you may call me Jake."

So much time had expired in the waiting room that Jake had to speak briefly and return to the city. He asked a few questions concerning why Al had received such a lengthy sentence and how much time he had remaining. Then Jake explained that the visit was mostly to get acquainted. Subsequently they would spend more time together. They exchanged a cordial farewell that ended their first encounter.

On the way back to the city, Jake surmised that if first impressions were lasting ones, he certainly was impressed with that fellow's demeanor. There is a little bad in the best of us and a little good in the worst, he thought. He waited with anticipation for the next visit. By now, his curiosity was definitely aroused.

Chapter 28

When Jake visited the prison again and on all subsequent visits, he was given special treatment. The officials agreed to a specific date and time for each visit until the interviews concluded. He spent only about ten or fifteen minutes in the waiting room, as he was given the same priority treatment given visiting lawyers.

They were allowed a separate visitor's room where they could sit at a table face to face without a barrier between them. A guard watched over them constantly. They were not allowed to shake hands or make any physical contact.

"Good morning, Al. We can get down to business today and hopefully make some progress."

"Good morning, Jake. I have been looking forward to seeing you again. Your visits will certainly make my day."

"Now tell me again, Al, just what exactly brought you to this place?" The answer was that Al was convicted of armed robbery, attempted murder, and conspiracy.

Jake took a deep breath and said, "Man, that is a hard pill to swallow. Are you comfortable with my questions? We can stop right now and end these interviews if you so desire."

"No, Jake, please continue. There is so much bottled up in me that sometimes I feel like I would rather die and get it all over with. I would be better off dead than in this place." He seemed to be fighting back tears.

At that point, Jake felt uneasy and asked the guard if both of them could have a cup of soda or water. The soda seemed to help both regain their composure.

Al said he was with two other guys. He was the only one caught. Because he refused to identify them, he was given so much time. "I would not rat on them. They are free and I am in here with my life ruined. We were returning from Atlantic City, New Jersey gambling and lost all of our money. One of my buddies decided to rob a store. They each had a gun and gave one to me. I never owned a gun. He told me that when the clerk sees a gun, he would hand over the money.

"We went into a convenience store to rob it. One stayed in the car with the motor running while two of us approached the clerk at the cash register. He pulled a gun from under the counter and aimed it at my head. My buddy shot him before he could shoot me. He fell behind the counter, and the friend with me snatched the gun from my hand, ran out, and jumped into the getaway car. The two took off without me. I ran down the street and rolled under a car to hide. I did not know where to go. I didn't even know where I was.

"I was caught. The clerk recovered and identified me. He actually thought I was the one who shot him. He was looking directly in my face when he was shot. I know I am still guilty because we were all together in the commission of a felony. That definitely is conspiracy."

In prison, Al told the journalist, inmates torture anyone they think is a snitch who would rat on a buddy.

There was an extremely long pause when neither of them said a word. Finally, Jake told Al that he was not there to judge him. Someone else had already done that. "You are paying for a crime you committed. Al, are you sure that you want to go on with these interviews?" Al agreed and that session ended.

Jake Spencer returned to his office with mixed emotions concerning that inmate. Almost all inmates have excuses for what they do. Was Al being entirely truthful? Because of everything he had just heard, Jake wanted to know more about Al's past.

CHAPTER 29

Much was revealed about Alfred's past, which proved to
be both interesting and disturbing. The journalist decided
to visit Alfred's mother as well.

She told him that she was born into a proud,
professional family who outwardly exhibited a style of
excellence before their peers. They were well thought of in
their church and community. Her father held a high office
in the Masonic Lodge and her mother was very active in
the Order of Eastern Stars. They were snobbish people
who looked down upon all unwed mothers and anyone
on welfare whom they considered lower class.

A family crisis arose when it became evident that
their daughter was indeed with child and not planning
to marry. Their daughter was a disgrace to them. What

would their neighbors and his business partners think of them? The young man's parents said that by no means would they sign for their son to marry at that age. He was expecting a scholarship. No shotgun wedding for their son. Within three or four months, they moved away.

Al's mother's snobbish family arranged for an abortion for their daughter. She refused, so they sent her away to a shelter for unwed mothers, telling anyone who asked that their daughter was at a boarding school. She was not allowed to call or write to them. In fact, they disowned her and moved away somewhere on the West Coast and resumed their way of life, possibly, never mentioning to their new friends and neighbors that they ever had a daughter.

CHAPTER 30

The story continued to unfold. The young mother gave birth to her son and refused to have him christened, because she was ashamed that she had him out of wedlock. When asked to have him blessed in the hospital, she said she would do it at her church. She had no church at the time. The shelter helped her find a place to live and affordable childcare for her baby.

The country was then engaged in World War II. Jobs were plentiful. Al's mother was able to obtain employment. She loved her child but felt guilty of some moral sin because she was not married.

His mother did not make friends in her neighborhood, because she thought they were saying bad things about her. For that reason, she refused to join a church. At one time, she became bitter at organized religions because of the treatment she received from her parents, who pretended to be religious people.

Her childcare giver noticed that she had no social life, and that could be bad for both mother and child. She was only seventeen at the time and needed to do more than go to work and come home and care for her baby.

The lady told her about the USO (United Service Organizations), which entertained servicemen in the area. "You need to get out of the house sometimes," she told Al's mother. The caregiver was a middle-aged woman who cared about Al's mother's well-being. She advised the young mother to respect herself at the USO. "Remember, you have one child. Think of how difficult it would be if you had two or three children with no husband "

Armed with that advice, Al's mother decided to become a volunteer hostess at the local USO. She met many people and really enjoyed being there, always remembering to be respectful at all times. The rule was never to leave the premises with any serviceman. She obeyed the rules.

One evening, while dancing with an attractive serviceman, he became attracted to her and she to him. They sipped soda together and talked. He wanted her phone number because he wanted to date her. She told him they would talk about it the next time she came to the USO, and she slowly drifted away from him.

She avoided going to the club for a few weeks, and when she returned, there was a note left there for her from the serviceman, telling her that he was being shipped overseas; he left his APO address. They corresponded by mail and married when he returned to the States. That is how she met Alfred's stepfather.

CHAPTER 31

Even though she did not connect with a local church, Alfred's mother allowed him to attend a Sunday school with a playmate who lived in the neighborhood.

He enjoyed being there and attended on a regular basis. Once in a while, he would stay for church service with his friend.

One Sunday, when an invitation to join the church was extended, Alfred walked to the altar and professed his desire to be a Christian. He was only seven at the time. He was asked if he believed that the Jesus he studied about at Sunday school was the Son of God. He was asked if he wanted to be a Christian?

The minister realized that young boy did not fully understand everything about Christianity, but he did not want to discourage the child from desiring a religious life. He allowed Al to repeat the prayer of salvation. The congregation gathered around the child and welcomed him into the Christian family. His mother was notified, and she allowed him to be baptized by immersion.

His mother remembered the scripture "Suffer the little children and forbid them not, for such is the kingdom of Heaven." Why those words came into her mind she did not know, for she had pulled away from the church because of the hypocritical actions of her parents.

When Jake returned to the prison, he had learned much about Al's family background. Now he wanted to know more about Alfred from the inmate himself. Al spoke of the time when he was young and his mother was out of the house. He went into her bureau drawer and was reading from her personal diary. When he heard her coming into the house, he hurriedly replaced it and returned to his bedroom.

When she noticed that the diary was not in the corner of her drawer in the exact spot were she hid it, she called Alfred because he was the only other one in the house at the time. He said he was not in her room. She slapped him very hard and called him a liar and a sneak. When she repeated the question, he admitted what he had done. "Were you reading my diary?" He admitted that was what he had been doing. "You did it and you lied to me," she told her son.

"You are a dishonest person and not to be trusted. I cannot trust you." She was furious and yelling. He did not forget that incident. He was humiliated by her words and never entered her bedroom again. He always remembered her calling him a liar and he was dishonest. Jake asked him why he did that. Al said that he knew it was wrong but could not give an answer as to why he wanted to read his mother's diary.

After her marriage, his mother gave birth to two other children. Her attitude seemed to have changed toward him after his little sisters were born. His stepfather showed no interest in Al's education and displayed no affection toward him. Al seemed to think that he was just in the way.

He often was beaten or humiliated for little things by his mother and sometimes by his stepfather, whose conversations with him were mostly reprimands. At home as a child, he was made to think that he could never do things right. He often wondered why he was ever born.

Jake noted that this was a troubled man. The cheerful, careful attitude that Alfred exhibited at their initial interview was just a façade. Now the inner feelings were beginning to surface.

CHAPTER 32

"Shall we continue?" Jake asked. Al hesitated and then said, "Please, Mr. Spencer, don't give up on me yet. We can make it. I promise you." That session ended, and Jake told Al he would see him in a few days.

When Jake returned again, he decided to inquire more deeply into Alfred's childhood. Something there must have influenced him to feel worthless. Alfred said that he and his mother were close until after her marriage. He seemed to think that her main reason to marry was to face the public and say, "Look at me. I have a husband." She was no longer an unwed mother.

His mother had rented a small house before she married. The stepfather moved into that house after the wedding and immediately took charge of everything. The couple didn't always get along. They argued a lot, but his mother was happy to have someone to help her pay bills and make her look respectable. His stepfather often stayed out late at night alone, and they argued about that.

Once, when Al's mother did hug him, the stepfather told her to "stop coddling that boy and making a sissy out of him. He is a man child and needs to grow up and be tough like a man." When referring to Al, he would always say, "This is my stepson, Al."

He remembered that when he was eight years old, his mother gave birth to her first daughter. His stepfather was ecstatic. They made such a fuss over that baby. You would think that Jesus Christ had entered their home. Relatives came from out of town just to see that precious little angel. Two years later, the second daughter was born, and the festivities were repeated. Alfred felt left out.

By ten years old, he began to run away from home. He would sleep on someone's porch overnight because he did not want to go home. Each time, his mother would notify the police. He did that about three times before a policeman who found him once came to their home and scared Alfred by telling him, "The next time you run away, I will take charge of you, and you would not want me to do that." He never ran away again.

Alfred's mother took a great deal of time teaching his little sisters to read. At the age of five, the first daughter was reading at a second-grade level. Mother bought books like Fun with Dick and Jane and Reading with Phonics. Her little girls learned to read many words phonetically at a very early age.

Al was a slow learner, and once, at about twelve years of age, his mother was helping with his homework. He could not read a certain word. His mother insisted that he do it. She embarrassed him by calling one of his little sisters, who immediately read the word without any effort. His mother made a big deal over the fact that he could not read as well as his little sister.

While in junior high school (later called middle school), he failed to turn in assignments and became disrespectful to some of his teachers. He was disruptive in class. Being frustrated and humiliated at home, he took out his frustrations on others at school. He became the class clown and was a hero among his peers. At least he was getting attention. His theory was, no matter what he would do, it would be the wrong thing. He probably lacked confidence in his ability to succeed scholastically.

His stepfather never went to school to talk with his teachers. It was always his mother's responsibility. Many days, she had to take off from work to speak with the principal about her son's behavior. One day, he and some of his friends were accused of placing a firecracker in a stray cat's rectum and setting it off. They did that on their way to school.

That was definitely animal cruelty. A child who saw the action reported the boys to the principal. His mother was summoned to school to witness the interrogation of the boys. Separately, each boy denied his involvement, naming one of the others. They were all guilty and were suspended for one week.

Alfred's mother and stepfather had jobs and wondered what the boys would get into, unsupervised for an entire week. She spoke with a counselor, who suggested enrolling him in an industrial boarding school out of town. At that time, it seemed to be the only solution to the problem of what to do about Alfred.

The school was a boarding school for troubled teenagers. His young parents were unaware of that at the time he was enrolled. He told of being thrown into a lake on the property by a group of boys because he could not swim. He said that somehow he maneuvered his way out of that pond and could swim from that day on.

The school also may have been a training camp for future penitentiary inmates. There were many really bad kids there. He got into trouble there as well. Once, when his mother visited him, she was told that he organized a gang at the school and he was their leader.

She withdrew him that day, stating that this was not the purpose of his being there. Back at home, there were gangs in the neighborhood. He was right back into an environment in which he could continue to get into trouble. Al at that time was not up to standards academically. Now that he was of high school age, they decided to enroll him in private school in Center City, which he attended daily. The cost was high, but they thought it was worth the money. This was an effort to separate him from gang members in their area.

At that session, Al told the journalist that some of those gang members from his old neighborhood were fellow inmates where he was confined. Alfred Spencer wondered if the fact that his unwed mother chose to keep her child was a wise thing to do. Both she and her young husband were not making mature decisions concerning the boy's upbringing.

The interviewer could clearly see that young Alfred should have been adopted by loving, caring parents who were willing to nurture him and give him the attention he needed. Something was definitely wrong with that picture.

The mother's choice of a mate and both of their attitudes toward the child could have been contributing factors in Alfred's behavior. The parents seemed to have behaved like children raising children. Jake Spencer dared not voice his opinion, for he was there to interview, not to judge.

CHAPTER 33

Back home again, Alfred the teenager completed his high school studies at the private school. It taught him the basics required for a high school diploma. There were no extracurricular activities involved, which may have been able to help him become a more well-rounded individual. His mother wanted to enroll him in a college. He refused to go.

He had returned home to an atmosphere of turmoil. His stepfather was an alcoholic and had an extramarital affair, a fact that Alfred was aware of and did not tell his mother. She drank a lot, but had not yet reached the dependency stage.

There was always an ample supply of whiskey in the house, which Alfred helped himself to when no one was around. He would pour out a certain amount and replace it with water, so that his parents would not notice any whiskey was missing. Eventually he became a teenage alcoholic.

One night, friends brought the drunken Al home, placed him on the front porch, and rang the bell before they drove away. His mother opened the door to see her glassy-eyed son sitting on the porch, slurring his speech, saying, "Hi, Mom. Your Al- is- a -bad boy." She helped him into the house. He crawled up the stairs and passed out on his bed. She never told her husband about that episode.

CHAPTER 34

At one of their sessions, the inmate confided extremely degrading things that happened to him after his arrest. He told of threats and beatings he received while police were trying to get him to name his accomplices. Those incidents were minor compared to what happened while being transported from the courthouse to the correctional facility, and treatment he received by inmates immediately after his arrival.

After the trial, a large number of prisoners were herded into a prison van. He had no idea how many were enclosed in there with no guard. Some were very large, foul-mouthed hoodlums who knew one another.

One asked his name, what crime he committed, and where he lived. "So that's where you live. I bet you think that you are better than us. How about that, boys? Let's get him." They pulled him to the floor and gang raped him right there in the back of the prison van.

When the van arrived at the prison, Alfred had to be assisted out of the van and taken to the prison infirmary for medical treatment. His first week there was his initiation period. Being of small stature, he had to endure overtures by some prison bullies. He became very frightened, being confined within the walls with those beastly people.

He attempted to remain in his cell but was forced to enter the exercise yard with other prisoners. There he was forced into a corner of the yard, where he was again raped by some of the men, while others stood around watching and laughing. It seemed that the guards may have looked the other way and let the inmates amuse themselves. That was not the first time something like that happened to him.

Jake asked Alfred how he managed to exist in a place like that for so many years. The answer was, "In here, you do what you have to do to survive." Al confided that one of the loud bullies asked Al if he was tired of those guys screwing around with him. He asked if Al wanted to put an end to what they were doing to him, and Alfred said yes.

"I can make them stop," the bully said.

Alfred understood what was being asked of him, and he reluctantly agreed to accept the proposal. They became a couple, and the gang rape ceased. The relationship was ongoing at the time of the interviews.

"Listen, Jake, in your story, please take a message from me to young boys out there. Tell them I said to study hard in school and get all the education they can. They must avoid drug and alcohol abuse, and above all obey the law. Crime will put them in a place like this. Hardened criminals confined in prisons are just waiting for young boys to get into prison and be sexually abused. Man, it's hard in here."

That was a very difficult session for Jake. He was shocked and shaken at the things he heard. He had begun the sessions and now wanted to end them at that point. However, he did continue with the interviews. The story would be interesting to his readers and could possibly deter some young boy away from criminal activities.

CHAPTER 35

During his young life at home, Alfred did remember some of the good times. He enjoyed bouncing up and down in the ocean waves on family trips to Atlantic City. He enjoyed family picnics in Fairmount Park. Not everything about his childhood was bad.

Christmas season was also a memorable time. His mother and stepfather joined a church in their neighborhood. There were always Christmas programs at church. Family and friends exchanged Christmas gifts. They enjoyed trimming the Christmas tree and singing carols. Friends and family visited, and there was always good food and plenty of whiskey and gin.

One year, he received a train set for Christmas. The engine smoked and the whistle blew. His parents had forgotten that he received a similar set a previous year, so he gave the old set to his friend, who had received only a couple articles of clothing and some candy, but no toys. His mother was a single mom, and that was all that she could afford. He never told his mother of that good deed.

During those times, his parents maintained their monthly parties at one another's homes, and there was always an abundance of alcoholic beverages on hand. Their party life was kept secret from church members. Children went along with them to the parties. Parents were frolicking in one section of the home, while the children played and enjoyed snacks and sodas in another.

Alfred did recall an isolated moment when his stepfather was pleased with something he did. He was babysitting his younger sister after school one day when she fell from her bicycle and hit her head on the curb outside of their home. Blood was gushing from the wound. He took her inside and placed a wet washcloth to her injury and called the police, who came immediately.

He and his sister were taken to the emergency ward of a local hospital Alfred gave them his mother's work telephone number. She was called and gave permission for her daughter to be treated, and then she rushed to the hospital.

At home that evening, when told of Al's actions, his stepfather patted him on the head and said, "That was a good thing you did today, boy." He was on cloud nine because he had met with their approval for something really nice that he had done. His mother often repeated the incident to friends and co-workers. He felt really good about himself for once.

He enlisted in the army. After basic training, he and a couple other soldiers went on a joyride with a jeep. He was driving, but was not authorized to drive the jeep at that time. There was an accident, and one of the soldiers was severely injured. Alcohol was found at the crash site. He was court-martialed and dishonorably discharged from the army.

After the discharge, he returned to Philadelphia and was hired by a company whose inventory included copper wire. Once when he visited his mother, he told her that some of the employees were stealing copper wire and selling it. She advised him not to become involved in that activity. He assured her that he was not. He lied.

While working, they would toss some of the wire over a fence behind the work yard. Late at night, after business hours, they returned with a small truck and collected the stolen items. When the employers noticed dwindling inventory, they hired a security agency. Those guys were caught red-handed and arrested on the spot.

Alfred's mother hired a lawyer, who successfully arranged for him not to go to jail by plea- bargaining and making restitution. He stated that had he gone to prison at that time and gotten a taste of what it was like to be incarcerated, maybe he would not be there talking to Jake that day.

Jake Spencer now had his story. He concluded his interviews at the prison and wished Alfred well in the future. He suggested that Alfred could contact him at a later date through the newspaper if he decided to go straight after his release. He anticipated a follow-up story. It was a bittersweet departure for both of them. The journalist felt that the inmate was a victim of a series of unfortunate circumstances in his young life; however, the decision to disobey the law was Alfred's alone.

CHAPTER 36

A number of years later, Jake Spencer, the ambitious journalist, was freelancing in Europe. By this time, he had partially dissociated himself from the newspaper.

A letter was forwarded to him from the United States. He did not immediately recognize the name of the sender, and he put it aside to read later. He was extremely busy at the time, and it did not appear to be urgent.

A few days later, he decided to catch up on what he considered less important correspondence. To his surprise, there was a letter from Alfred, who was out of prison on parole. He went into detail concerning numerous problems he had encountered in his attempt to obtain meaningful employment, due to his incarceration.

He was extremely grateful for the time the reporter had spent with him during those difficult moments when he was baring his soul to a stranger. Alfred had not seen his story in any publication and was concerned about it.

He also told of an interviewer interested in helping young men with problems get a fresh start in life. On his application, he stated that he had served a prison term and was then eager to get on with his life. However, he failed to include the attempted murder charge for which he was convicted.

The interviewer was smiling and extremely congenial before asking Alfred what those charges were. When he was told that a gun was involved and Alfred was charged with attempted murder, the man's demeanor changed abruptly. He began shuffling papers on his desk and seemed to be trying to find the right words to say. Finally, he told Alfred that he presented himself well and it was great that he was seeking to improve himself, and should he decide to hire Alfred, he would give him a call. The call never came. Other places of employment offering adequate wages also put him on the "Do not call us, we will call you" list.

In order to support himself, he had to accept low-paying jobs with no chance for advancement. He barely existed, working for minimum wage. He was determined not to do anything that would send him back to prison again.

The situation he was in was one that many released prisoners face. Alfred realized that society frowns upon those who have committed crimes. He understood the reason why. Still, he had no intention of repeating those crimes. He would die before he would let anyone send him back to prison. The conditions there were just that bad.

Jake knew that former inmates often return to crime out of frustration, due to similar situations. He browsed through the rather lengthy letter and realized that this ex-convict was making an honest effort to go straight. When he found time, he penned a short note, explaining that he was on assignment out of the country and would contact Al when he returned to the United States.

Six months passed, and Jake came home. When he attempted to reach Alfred, the letter was returned to him marked "undeliverable." He assumed that things got too rough for Alfred and he may have returned to his old habits and was caught.

During the Christmas season, another letter was forwarded to Jake via the Weekly Express. This time it explained why no one could contact him for a while. A former prison inmate, out on parole had been stalking him and attempting to resume their intimate relationship.

Alfred was afraid of the man and was avoiding him. He finally felt safe where he was living and was no longer being pursued.

Jake arranged to meet Alfred at a public place. The meeting proved to be most interesting, and a second round of meetings began. Jake did not completely trust Al because of his criminal background, so their meetings were in public places. He did not give Alfred his home address. His family always knew where he would be when meeting with the inmate.

CHAPTER 37

Alfred's mother visited often while he was incarcerated. She deposited money in his prison account for cigarettes, stamps, and other essentials. Upon his release, he stayed with her and his two sisters. She was separated from her husband, who wanted no association with an ex-convict. Alfred's living arrangements with his mother were temporary until he was able support himself.

He had a drinking problem and attended AA meetings on a regular basis, for he was a recovering alcoholic. He had to stand before everyone and state his name and the fact that he was an alcoholic. He had to tell the number of days (or months) he had been sober, followed by a round of applause. Whenever he had a desire to take a drink, he had a buddy to call. They encouraged one another to stick with the program.

The AA helped him to find employment. The pay was inadequate, but he was able to manage by buying his clothing and shoes at a Salvation Army thrift store. He admitted that there were times when he was tempted to shoplift, especially in a grocery store when he was hungry. Then he had flashbacks about prison and had second thoughts.

One day, a customer in the convenience store where he worked handed him a business card and said, "Call me." He wondered why he should call that man. When he did, the man told him how he had noticed that Alfred seemed to be a dedicated worker with a great attitude. He asked why Alfred did not try to get a better job.

He told the man that he was doing the very best he could under the circumstances. He told the man all about his conviction and prison term, including the fact that he was out on parole. The man wanted to meet with Alfred to help him.

Chapter 38

The business man was Mr. Frederickson, a devout Christian who led a youth group in his church. He was greatly impressed with Alfred. He talked with him at length and saw great potential in him. He wanted to help Alfred.

Mr. Fredrickson owned a company that installed hardwood flooring and carpeting. He hired Alfred as an apprentice, with a salary a little more than he was earning at the convenience store. As he mastered his skill, the salary increased considerably. Before long, he was able to rent a small apartment and improve his lifestyle.

Alfred became a member of his employer's church and soon was singing in the choir. He had a wonderful tenor voice. While engaged in criminal activities, he had strayed from church doctrine. The double standards of his parents discouraged him.

As time passed, he began to counsel troubled youth in the church and in the surrounding neighborhood. He arranged for hard-core troubled young men who seemed to be headed for big trouble to be taken on trips to a state prison as a wake-up call to encourage them to change their destructive behavior.

Alfred introduced a few with substance abuse problems to the AA program. He told them of mistakes that he had made and the consequences of alcohol abuse and criminal behavior. He helped a number of young teens to live better lives.

He became attracted to a lovely young lady who sang in the church choir. Alfred feared rejection because of his criminal background. They often exchanged a casual smile at one another.

His past was no secret to the congregation. He was proud of the fact that his sordid past was behind him. He revealed his feelings for the lady to Mr. Fredrickson, who casually mentioned the fact to her parents.

The parents admired Alfred and had no objections to his seeing their daughter. When he finally approached the young lady to ask her out for a dinner date, she smiled and responded, "I thought you would never ask."

They became very fond of one another and dated occasionally while she was in nursing school. He did not date anyone else during that time. After her graduation, they began making wedding plans and had a very large church wedding and reception, financed by her parents with a little help from the church. Most of their church members attended the affair.

They purchased a modest home just outside of Philadelphia and invited Jake to visit with them. When he arrived, he was greeted at the door by a smiling Alfred, who immediately said, "Mr. Spencer, I want you to meet my wife.

The journalist spontaneously replied, "You still can call me Jake." That remark precipitated a burst of laughter from the two. It was a reminder of their first meeting many years ago.

His wife Joan was charming. The home was tastefully furnished and had beautiful hardwood flooring. 'Did you lay this flooring?" Jake asked.

"He certainly did, and I am so proud of my husband," Al's wife answered for him. All of the good things that were happening in his life resulted from someone having faith in his ability and giving him a chance.

A short time later, they had another visitor. He was a well-dressed, elderly man with a charming gray mustache. Alfred introduced the new arrival. He was

Mr. Frederickson, his benefactor, who soon told how impressed he was with his new employee.

Mr. Frederickson envisioned helping Alfred start his own business. He stated that there was enough business out there for both of them. He welcomed the competition, especially if it came from Alfred.

"We have good news," Joan announced. "There is a little one on the way."

Alfred beamed as congratulations were extended. He told them that he planned to give his child all of the love and encouragement that he wished his parents had given him.

Jake admitted that he had not published the original story because he was waiting for a follow-up. Soon he would begin working on that follow-up. They spent a wonderful evening together.

Chapter 39

Mr. Frederickson did in fact assist Jake in setting up a small business. He advertised locally in his neighborhood for customers. Some church members began using his services and referring him to others. Alfred's business was growing. After a few years, he rented space in a strip mall, where he stored his supplies and had his office. He bought two work vans, hired an accountant and a couple of young men from the area to work for him. He trained his new employees and even invited them to his home at times.

Will, one of his workers, was a high school dropout. He seemed to be an ambitious worker. He told Alfred of his petty theft record. He was jailed for that and decided to stay out of trouble, because he now had two small children to support. The other worker was Sam, who had graduated from high school and was recently honorably discharged from military service.

Alfred stressed the importance of honesty to his employees, particularly because they were working in people's homes. It was imperative that they did not touch any of their customer's personal property. The success of the company depended on their reliability. He stated that until he had complete trust in them, he would be watching them closely.

Alfred had a great family life. They enjoyed celebrating birthdays and thought it would be nice to surprise his employee, Will, on his birthday. They chose a workday, and it would be a come-as-you-are party, so that no one had to get dressed. It was a great way to surprise Will.

On the day of the party, Alfred and his men went to work as usual, all rode in one van. While working in one of the bedrooms and trying to complete the job, Will announced that he had a sudden urge to use the bathroom. Alfred was involved in trying to complete the job. He told Will to use bathroom down the hall because access to the one in the room in which they were working was blocked. Alfred and Sam continued with their work.

Will returned and joined the other two, who were busy laying carpet in the room. When the job was completed, they headed for home. By that time, guests had arrived for the surprise party. Alfred told them that he would stop by his house before driving Will and Sam home, because he had to pick a few things. Will insisted that he needed to go right home because he had something to do. Alfred said okay and continued driving to his own home.

Joan greeted them at the door, yelling, "Come quickly, I have a problem." All three men started toward the house, when Will began digging in his pockets and said he may have dropped his wallet in back of the van. Alfred told him to hurry back because Joan may need their help. As Will was returning to the van, the others thought it was great. They would join the guests and shout "Surprise!" as the birthday boy entered the house.

When he approached the front door, someone opened it and they all yelled, "Surprise!" He stood motionless with mouth agape. It seemed that he did not know what to say. Joan noted that they really did surprise him. "Just see the look on his face." The party began.

Later, someone asked if Will had found his wallet. He hesitated for a moment and replied, "Oh yes, I have it." The question appeared to have startled Will for a brief moment.

They played music, served food, and presented Will with presents. He said repeatedly, "You guys should not be doing this."

One hour had passed when there was a knock on the front door and a loud voice yelling, "Police, open the door." A bewildered Alfred approached the policeman and asked what it was all about. The officers had a warrant to search the premises because someone had filed a complaint against his company. "You are accused of theft and conspiracy which may involve a felony charge depending on the value of the stolen goods."

The wife where they had been working returned home shortly after Alfred and his employees completed their last job. She noticed a very expensive heirloom ring was missing. It was on her dresser in a small case. She always kept it in plain view and never saw a need to hide it. She immediately called her husband and they filed a complaint before the ring could be disposed of.

Alfred could not believe what he was hearing. His wife Joan began crying uncontrollably. Everyone there was searched. The house was thoroughly searched, without telling anyone exactly what they were looking for.

One of the officers asked for key to their work van. He retuned, jubilantly announcing, "I found it." Wrapped in tissue paper, in a drawer of Alfred's tool chest, he found the missing ring. Alfred told them that he had no idea it was there. He and his employees were read their rights and arrested. They were booked, photographed, and fingerprinted at the local police station. Then they were questioned individually. Each stated he had no knowledge of the theft.

Alfred had not yet completed his parole period. He was told that if found guilty, he would be returned to the state prison. They assumed that Alfred was involved in some way.

Mr. Frederickson was called, and he obtained a lawyer. Alfred cried continuously. He knew that he did not steal that ring and had no knowledge of the theft. Since Will acted suspiciously, he was sure that Will was the guilty one. He and Sam were together the entire time they were in that house. When Will left them to go to the bathroom, he must have taken that ring.

Mr. Frederickson and his minister were character witnesses for Alfred. They could not speak for the other two. The men were released on bail until the trial date. When questioned about his absence to retrieve his wallet, Will stated that all he did was pick up his wallet from the floor where he had apparently dropped it. Then he returned to the house. According to the police, any one of the three could be the guilty one. They suspected Alfred, because of his criminal record and the fact that the ring was found in his tool box.

Chapter 40

News of the stolen ring reached the local newspapers, mentioning Alfred's incarceration in state prison. Both Sam and Alfred were positive that Will was the thief but were unable to prove it. In the eyes of the legal system, all were co-conspirators.

Alfred's wife and child returned home with her family because the neighbors became less friendly. She stopped eating, and she cried all of the time. She loved her husband and wanted to believe he was innocent. She became distraught and refused to leave her room. Her mother had to care for both Joan and her little daughter. Soon she was diagnosed as having a nervous breakdown and checked into a hospital.

Alfred could no longer continue with his business. He sold his two vans and began living on his savings. He signed a quitclaim, giving his wife sole ownership of their home. He was ashamed to attend his church because he felt people were talking about him.

In fact, all that had transpired began to affect him mentally as well. There always remained the possibility of his being returned to prison. That devastated him. Under no circumstances did he ever want to return to prison life. Memories of his being there still gave him nightmares at times.

Alfred visited Will and tried unsuccessfully to convince him to admit his guilt. Will said nobody could prove that he did it. There was nothing more Alfred could do. Slowly Alfred seemed to be sinking into a state of depression.

The day of the trial arrived. The courtroom was crowded. Because they lived in a small town, he and his company name had become the talk of the town. The victims of the crime arrived early. They sat chatting with their lawyer. Alfred's minister and his in-laws were present and sat together. Members of the local press appeared with their cameras.

The court clerk said, "All rise." The judge took his place on the bench. Alfred's case was called. His lawyer stood and stated that his client had not yet arrived. Later, when it was apparent that Alfred still was not there, the judge ordered a bench warrant for Alfred's arrest.

Unable to reach Alfred by phone, his lawyer went to his client's home. Alfred lived outside of Philadelphia. Driveways were behind some the houses and gave access to garages in the rear of the homes. Not receiving an answer to the doorbell, the lawyer walked to the back of the house where he spotted Alfred's car parked in his driveway. The motor was running. A hose was connected from the exhaust pipe to inside the car. He saw his client slumped behind the wheel. Alfred was dead. Two sealed letters lay beside him.

Those letters were read at a subsequent trial for the remaining suspects. To his wife, Alfred wrote; *"I love you very much and pray you will recover very soon. Circumstantial evidence may send me back to prison if Will does not admit what he did. Sam and I knew nothing about the theft. Will knows that he is the guilty one. I suffered extreme punishment in prison for something that I did. I refuse to return there for something I did not do. May God forgive me for what I am about to do."*

To Will, Alfred wrote: *"I hired you knowing that you had a record because I also had one. I trusted you and you betrayed me. You know that you stole that ring. Admit it. You destroyed my business and my family.*

You caused my wife to have a **nervous** ***breakdown. I will not return to prison for something that you did. My death will be on your conscience for as long as you live. I pray God will forgive you."***

Both letters were read before Will took the stand in his own defense. He sat there visibly shaken and tearfully admitted his guilt. He said that he stole the ring and had it in his pocket. Afraid that he would drop it, he made an excuse to return to the van and placed it in the tool chest drawer, planning to get it later. At the trial, he was sentenced and Sam went free.

Will was led away from the courtroom, sobbing loudly and yelling, "Al is dead and it is all my fault! I am so sorry." He continued to say, "It is all my fault that he is dead." His voice gradually faded away as he was being led down the long corridor. A few months later, while still in custody, Will was eventually admitted to a psychiatric hospital.

Among those who spoke at Alfred's funeral were three college students, a number of high school students, and members of the youth group with whom he had been working. All spoke of how Alfred had helped them to live a better life, urging them to stay away from criminal activities.

Mr. Fredrickson and Jake Spencer also spoke and reminded those present how difficult it could be for ex-offenders to accomplish what Alfred had done, and his death was most unfortunate. His life came to a tragic end. They agreed that he did not deserve what had finally happened to him.

Jake Spencer stated that was not the follow-up he expected to conclude in his human-interest story on Alfred's life. There was not a dry eye in that church as the minister's closing remark was, "Let the good work that he has done speak for him." The mourners slowly left the sanctuary as a soloist sang softly, "If I can help somebody as I pass along, If I can help somebody with a word or song — then my living will not be in vain."

LaVergne, TN USA
29 August 2009
156215LV00005B/2/P